~~~~~~~

C000227612

FATAL

TRIBUTE

~~~~~~~~~~~~~~~~~~

The Seacastle Mysteries

Book 3

PJ Skinner

ISBN 978-1-913224-46-2

Parkin Press
INDEPENDENT PUBLISHER

Cover design by Mariah Sinclair

Discover other titles by PJ Skinner

The Seacastle Mysteries

Deadly Return (Book 1)

Eternal Forest (Book 2)

Toxic Vows (Book 4)

Mortal Mission: A Murder mystery on Mars

Written as Pip Skinner

The Green Family Saga (written as Kate Foley)

Rebel Green (Book 1)

Africa Green (Book 2)

Fighting Green (Book 3)

The Sam Harris Adventure Series

Fool's Gold (Book 1)

Hitler's Finger (Book 2)

The Star of Simbako (Book 3)

The Pink Elephants (Book 4)

The Bonita Protocol (Book 5)

Digging Deeper (Book 6)

Concrete Jungle (Book 7)

Also available as box sets

Go to the PJ Skinner website for more info and to
purchase paperbacks directly from the author:
https://www.pjskinner.com

Dedicated to my sister Amy

Chapter 1

Whoever invented wind shelters for seaside promenades should be given a medal. I suspect the Victorians had something to do with it. They were geniuses at building eccentric islands that served as places to congregate, eat, drink or play music. Wind shelters were an extension of this idea. Small oases giving respite from the constant breeze and common squalls of the British seaside. Unfortunately, the wind shelters in Seacastle now accommodated the local winos during the day and the pushers at night. However, the gale had cleared the promenade of all but the hardiest souls, so I had one all to myself, sheltered from the elements and with a view of the wind farm standing stark against banks of grey cloud. I sat back against the bench and watched the herring gulls huddling along the pebble banks, their beaks pointing into the wind.

As I gazed into the distance, I became aware that my mobile telephone was vibrating in my jacket pocket, but I hadn't heard it. The ring tone could not compete with the din made by the howling wind and crashing waves. I put it to my ear without checking the screen, a habit from my recently expired Luddite era, when I had a bog-standard Nokia instead of the splendid smartphone I now owned.

'Honestly, Tanya. Are you going deaf? I've tried to reach you at least three times already.'

I rolled my eyes. My older sister Helen, arbiter of all good behaviour and social mores, had a habit of getting right up my nose. She had a good heart, if you could find your way past all the strictures, but sometimes I wished for a Hallmark sister, all hugs and hearts with a non-judgemental and forgiving nature.

'Sorry. I'm out here in a gale and I didn't hear my phone.'

'I've got news.'

'I can't hear you.'

'Go home and call me from there.'

'I'll go back to the Grotty Hovel and ring you back.'

'Don't call it that. It's a perfectly nice house and—'

To my relief the signal died. I knew exactly what she was about to say; how my ex-husband George had given me the house when we divorced out of the goodness of his heart. She thought I behaved like a spoilt brat when I moved into the two-up-two-down terraced house I had swapped for my glamorous villa in the outskirts of Seacastle. But I love the house now, in all its cosy, shabby chic, vintage glory. The villa had been a sterile beige object, hollow and echoing with minimalism. I had imagined it to be stylish at the time, but soulless would be closer to the truth. I had stuffed the Grotty Hovel with articles from my vintage shop, Second Home, some of which I had planned to sell eventually, a flexible time period which could stretch out to infinity.

I emitted a sigh which got lost in the gale, and trudged back to my house, loose hairs from my bun whipping against my face. When I got to my front door, I dropped my keys on the doorstep, which did not improve my humour. I loved to ruminate in the wind shelter on my day off, and being berated by my sister for some imagined failing did not appeal. The door creaked open and I thought about oiling the hinges for the umpteenth time. My cat, Hades, raised his head from the sofa and examined my windswept state before lowering it again and drifting back off to sleep. His lack of interest was par for the course. He still wouldn't let me stroke him, although he would share the sofa with me now instead of leaping off in a mad panic.

I could visualise Helen's impatience growing as she waited for me to call her back, but that didn't stop me from making myself a cup of coffee first. I needed bolstering before I could face the charges. Finally, I could put it off no longer. I lowered myself onto the sofa, carefully avoiding dripping coffee on it, or alienating Hades by giving him a fright. He opened one eye and glowered at me, but he did not move. I resisted the temptation to run my hand over his shimmering black fur and scratch his pointy ears. My phone rang just as I reached for it, making me jump.

'Hello?'

'Why haven't you called me back yet?'

'Sorry, the road flooded and I had to take a detour.'

A loud sigh.

'No it didn't. I don't know why you bother lying to me. Anyway, I have great news.'

'I'm on tenterhooks, honest.'

'Hmm. Well, I'm coming to Seacastle.'

'That's nice. Will you pop in to see me?'

'I expect so. I'll be living next door.'

'Next door?'

'Yes. Isn't that great?'

I swallowed and tried to keep my tone neutral.

'Are you moving house?'

'No, silly. I told you already that Olivia won the regional tribute act final last month. Well, the Nationals are being held in the theatre at Seacastle. She looked on Airbnb and discovered that the house next door to you has just come online. We have booked it for a few weeks. Isn't that wonderful?'

'It's amazing,' I said. 'It will be great to have you both so near to me. Mouse will be thrilled.'

Mouse, my sort-of stepson, son of my ex-husband, lived with me in the Grotty Hovel. Helen did not approve of Mouse, but he had had a crush on Olivia since their last visit. I had visions of a cat among the pigeons, and I did not have Hades in mind. Mouse had developed into a bit of a dreamboat, and I had to warn him not to break the hearts of my customers or their daughters as we would soon have none left. He had been through a delinquent stage in his teens, including a night in the clink for carjacking, but he had since reformed and learned to hack websites instead. He had transformed me from Luddite Queen to Internet Princess and installed Wi-Fi in both my house and shop. I could easily imagine Mouse's crush getting reciprocated. Every girl loves a bad boy. Helen would be livid.

'She'll be far too busy to see much of Mouse,' said Helen, sniffing. 'How is your cat? Does he still hate you?

Maybe he'll come next door and see me. After all, it is his original home.'

'Hades doesn't hate me. He's just sensitive.'

'Like George? Anyway, I must be getting on. I'll text you a time for our arrival when I'm near. It's going to be lots of fun.'

I'm not sure what sort of fun she had in mind when she said this, but I had my suspicions. Helen's idea of fun was a four-hour Wagner opera on the radio. I tried to have things in common with her, but she had taken George's side in the divorce and that made it hard for me to like her anymore.

Later that afternoon, Harry called me to see if I wanted to do a clearance with him. He was the nearest thing I had to a boyfriend and I adored him, but somehow, we always seemed to find reasons to delay our relationship. We still managed to get on like a house on fire on our good days, and that gave me hope we would muddle through somehow.

'Ms Bowe? Can I rely on your company tomorrow? I have a house clearance on the outskirts of Chichester.'

'It would be my pleasure, Mr Fletcher. At what time shall I await the chariot?'

'Nine-thirty. There's no point trying to get there during the rush hour.'

'I'll be on the doorstep.'

'See you tomorrow then.'

After he rang off, I lay back and held the phone over my heart and allowed happiness to flood over me. The days I spent doing clearances with Harry were right up there with my best. Mouse came downstairs and spotted me.

'Wait, don't tell me. Harry just called you?'

'How did you know?'

'Honestly, you two are like shy teenagers. When are you going to get together?'

'We are together.'

'Philosophically or metaphysically?'

'It's none of your business. We're doing our best.'

'Hmm. So you say. Are you doing a clearance?'

'Chichester.'

'Can I come?'

'No.'

He grinned.

'You two,' he said. 'I could get jealous.'

'Don't be silly. Guess who called earlier?'

'George?'

'No, Helen. She and Olivia are coming to stay next door.'

'Next door? Isn't that the house where you found Hades?'

'That's right. They've made it into an Airbnb.'

'Did Helen leave Martin?'

'Don't be silly. Martin has to stay at home for his work. Olivia's singing in that tribute show they're putting on in the Pavilion. Somebody left at the last minute and they needed another girl.'

When are they arriving?'

'Far too soon.'

Chapter 2

The next morning, I waited outside in the rain for Harry to arrive. Several damp-looking herring gulls sat huddled together on the roof of the house opposite mine, their bright yellow beaks shiny with water. I always found the way they stared at me intimidating, like sea vultures waiting for me to keel over. One of them opened his beak to start calling and they all joined in like a chorus at the opera.

Harry's van turned the corner into my street, streaked with rivulets of rain funnelling through the dirt. He refused to clean it, claiming that rubbing the dirt off scratched the paint, but I found it hard to believe. My Mini sat in a resident's parking space outside my house, plumply pleased with itself, its newly waxed exterior repulsing the rain drops. I resisted the temptation to pat it like a dog and gave Harry a wave.

He stopped in the street and I squeezed between the parked cars, getting my trousers wet. He flung open the passenger door.

'Your steed awaits, Milady.'

'I see you camouflaged it with mud.'

'I've got to keep in practice,' he said. 'You never know when my battle craft will be required.'

I grinned. His time in the services remained shrouded in mystery, but I had recently learned from Mouse that the winged dagger tattoo on Harry's back showed he had spent time in the special forces. Probably S.A.S. I longed to ask Harry about it, but he gave out information in small packages when he felt like it and not when asked. I couldn't imagine how to bring up the subject without making him clam up like a bank vault on a timer.

I put on a mix of classic rock and roll and enjoyed the drive past the hedgerows of whitebeam, hawthorn, rowan and maple with their bright green leaves gleaming in the rain. We passed through Arundel and I strained to catch a glimpse of the castle, a thousand years of history beguiling me with its turrets and winding walls. I wondered if they had any items in their basement they wanted to offload.

The hum of the traffic and the swish of the wind screen wipers put me to sleep and I woke with a jolt as Harry stopped at some traffic lights not far from our destination.

'Welcome back,' he said. 'You were snoring like a trooper.'

'I don't snore.'

'If you say so.'

I peered out at the pretty streets as we made our way to King George's Square. Chichester had been voted as Britain's best place to live, and the prices had since shot up, making it unobtainable for anyone who fancied it. Trend setters had tried to make Seacastle into the next

Brighton, and the best British seaside town to move to, but people had turned up their noses. I crossed my fingers it would last a little longer. I liked having the beach to myself and to walk the whole promenade without meeting anyone under sixty-five.

We pulled into an alley leading to a private garage. Harry put a note in the windscreen of the van with his mobile phone number, telling the owner where we were if they needed access. The house we were clearing formed part of a terrace and as we neared it in the drizzle, I could see a large pile of objects on the pavement outside. The mizzle made it hard to see what they were until we came closer. Then I realised the pile had been made up of furniture thrown randomly together without care or order. Some of the pieces appeared to have been damaged by their treatment.

Harry ran up the steps to the front door and a man coming out with a side table almost knocked him back down them.

'You want to watch yourself,' he said, but then backed off when he saw Harry stiffen.

'I'm here to do the house clearance,' said Harry. 'But I see you've started without me.'

His tone held no amusement. The man placed the table on the top steps.

'The boss told me to throw it out,' he said, 'He wants to gut the place so he can convert it into flats.'

'And when did he ask you to do this?'

'Today. He's inside.'

'Excuse us,' said Harry, and beckoned me inside.

I mumbled apologies as I pushed past the man and entered the house. In front of me, a mahogany staircase snaked up to the next floor, at least three metres above the one we were on. Long sash windows framed by heavy velvet drapes let in bright summer sunlight which flooded the hall and drawing room at the front of the building. The grandeur of the house took my breath away. I couldn't believe they intended to gut it. The furniture from the ground floor had already been removed and the thick carpets had deep indentations where it used to rest. A sparrow flew around the drawing room, crashing into the window panes, desperate to escape.

A heavy-set man came down the stairs, his eyebrows drawn together in fury.

'And who the hell are you?' he said, sticking his face up close to Harry's.

'My name is Harry Fletcher and—'

'Major?' said the man, and his whole demeanour changed. 'Holy crap. I didn't recognise you out of uniform.'

He pulled in his tummy and stood to attention, snapping off a sharp salute. Harry shook his head.

'At ease, Corporal Rivers. We're not in the army now.'

The man stuck out his meaty paw and shook Harry's hand.

'It's great to see you again. And who's this? Your A.D.C?' he said, leering at me.

'Tanya's my business associate.'

'If you say so, sir.'

He looked me up and down.

'Aren't you scared of hanging around with the S.A.S?' he said.

I opened my mouth to say something funny, but Harry put a hand on my shoulder.

'Don't answer that,' he said. 'Why don't you show Corporal Rivers the pieces you'd like to keep, and he and his buddy will take them to our van for us.'

Nobody listening could have mistaken the seemingly casual suggestion for anything other than a command. Rivers directed me upstairs and I tried to concentrate as I scanned the contents of the rooms for anything I could sell on. Most of the furniture upstairs had been abandoned due to its unfashionable era. There were large Victorian wardrobes in dark varnish which would never fit into a modern sized room. Also, useless three legged tables which would fall over every time you put a cup of tea on one side. A few marble-stemmed lamps could have passed muster, but they all had chipped exteriors that suggested the presence of excitable small dogs or children running riot upstairs.

I shook my head at the drab selection, but then I noticed a Persian carpet in one of the bedrooms. It had a worn patch at the entrance, but the rest looked as if it could offer another hundred years of service. I could see it in the sitting room of the Grotty Hovel. It would cover almost the whole floor area.

'Can you roll that up for me?' I said.

'Would you like to be rolled inside it, like Cleopatra?' said Rivers, winking at me. 'My name's Baz, by the way.'

'No thanks. But thanks for the thought, Baz,' I said.

They carried the rolled-up carpet downstairs between them, as it dipped and sagged like a recalcitrant python. Outside, on the pavement, Harry had dismantled most of the pile of furniture and divided it into two parts. I tried not to review the contents of the broken pile. No use crying over spilt milk and all that. There were a pair of nice his-and-hers Parker Knoll armchairs with matching footstools that screamed Grace Wong at me. She and her husband Max ran an expensive antique shop, up the posh end of the same high street where I had my shop. She liked to cherry-pick my hauls and sell the best pieces at double the price she paid me. I never objected, as she paid in cash, something in short supply.

Once the van had been loaded, Harry shook hands with the men and exchanged phone numbers with Baz Rivers. They had a quick private conversation once I had got into the van. I could see them in the wing mirror, gesticulating and screwing their faces up. They didn't appear to be quarrelling, but Harry's expression, as he walked to the van, looked like thunder. He gesticulated towards the back.

'I don't know why we bother sometimes,' he said.

'I got a nice carpet for the sitting room.'

'But the rest will hardly cover the fuel. This is my livelihood, you know.'

'It's mine too. I'm just trying to look on the bright side. What on earth did Rivers say to you?'

'I don't know what you mean.'

'You've been acting weirdly since you talked to him. We often have abortive trips. You don't usually let it get to you.'

Harry's grip on the steering wheel had made his knuckles go white. He muttered something I didn't catch.

'What?'

'It's a family problem,' he said.

He had never mentioned his family before. I don't know why, but I assumed he was an orphan like me, and he'd never laid claim to any siblings.

'The worst kind,' I said, meaning to sympathise. 'Did I tell you my awful sister Helen is moving in next door. Nightmare.'

He turned to look at me, his face hard.

'You need to repair your relationship with your sister. You have no idea what a real problem looks like. Sometimes you're just a spoilt brat.'

Chastened, I bit my lip. He had never spoken to me like that before. We had always got on like a house on fire. I tried to control the wave of self-pity swamping me. We drove home in silence. Harry did not call me after he dropped me off. Normally, even our worse tiffs only lasted an hour or two before one of us capitulated. This time, an implacable silence had reverberated from him on our journey home. I knew better than to telephone him. Harry would explain when he felt ready.

Chapter 3

The Vintage coffee shop on the first floor of Second Home sustained my business by a thread. Summer was low season in the antique trade. People were too busy going on holiday and visiting their families to spend time indoors looking at relics from other eras. Mouse ran the café with humour and charm, and his regency good looks attracted many customers who came specially for a flirt. Despite the good business we did in the café, it did not generate sufficient income to cover the expenses generated by both the Second Home and the Grotty Hovel. I needed to find other ways to bring in income. Perhaps I could rent out the office again, although that didn't turn out quite as I had expected the last time.

I had spent the morning pondering my options when Jasmine Smith entered the shop. She and I had met several times in the past, including at Melanie Conrad's funeral. Jasmine had trained as a photographer. She worked freelance and often did spreads for the local newspaper. She had a genuine talent and enthusiasm which shone through her work, especially her portraits. When she didn't find me on the ground floor, she came upstairs to look for me. A broad grin lit up her face when she saw me mooching on the banquette in the window of the Vintage.

'Hello, stranger,' she said. 'I can't believe I haven't been to visit your shop or café before. It's gorgeous.'

'The Vintage café is a legacy of Mel's. She's the one who suggested it, you know.'

'I didn't,' she said, pulling a strand of black hair off her face. 'Why didn't you download those photos I put in the Dropbox for you? The ones of Mel's funeral.'

'I'm sorry. I completely forgot, to be honest. We were so confused by the whole case and all the possible connotations of the evidence.'

Her face came into focus and I noticed her stunning eyes. I realised they were different colours. Why hadn't I noticed before? She did wear sunglasses a lot. I tried not to stare, looking instead at my notebook for inspiration.

'Heterochromia,' she said. 'It's hereditary.'

'They're quite stunning.'

'Thanks. You got the murderer in the end. Thank goodness. I was so surprised when I found out who had committed the murders.'

'I got a shock myself when I had a gun shoved in my face.'

Jasmine roared with laughter.

'That would be hard to forgive.'

'What brings you here today? Can I offer you a glass fisherman's float or a peacock chair?'

She frowned.

'I'm not a big fan of antiques, to be honest. I came to see if you had time to work with me on a freelance contract I've been awarded.'

'What sort of work?'

'Did you hear that the National Talent Competition Finals are to be held in the Pavilion Theatre?'

I tried to hide a smile.

'What's that smile for? Are you competing?'

'Goodness no. My sister's daughter Olivia is a talented singer songwriter and she won her regional final as Carole King. They're moving into the Airbnb next door to me for the duration.'

'Wow. Congratulations. Well, that's one interview sorted.'

'Interview?'

'Yes, I'm contracted to take portraits of the finalists for posters and media coverage and I need someone to interview the finalists and to write filler pieces for possible syndication. Is that something you fancy doing?'

'Of course. I'd love to.'

'If it's okay with you, I'd like to go halves on the fee. They're paying pretty well, and the more articles they take, the more they pay.'

'That sounds fantastic; if you're sure?'

'I'm sure. When can you start?'

'Just let me know who to interview first and I'll do some research, or at least Mouse will.'

'Mouse?'

'My step-son. George's boy. He makes good coffee too.'

Hearing his name, Mouse came over to us.

'That's me,' he said. 'What would you like? The cake of the week is Mocha, if you're hungry.'

'Mocha? And our waistlines?' I said.

'Who's talking about diets?' said Ghita Chowdhury, mounting the stairs.

I had not heard her coming in either. She and Roz Murray are my dearest friends. As well as working for the council, Ghita runs exercise classes under the name Fat Fighters Club, an institution in Seacastle. She also makes the cakes for the Vintage, which might be seen as a conflict of interests, by a jaundiced eye.

'God forbid,' said Jasmine. 'I've got a metabolism like a combi-boiler. Super-efficient. No diets for me.'

'Wait 'til you're our age,' I said. 'Menopause and metabolism are not friends. Ghita, this is Jasmine. She's a photographer and I'm going to be helping her at the Talent Competition by writing articles. Can you do any extra time this week?'

'Nice to meet you. I'm not sure. I promised Rohan and Kieron I'd help them move in.'

'Move in? They found somewhere for the restaurant? Why didn't you tell me?'

'Because I came straight here to tell you. They agreed the purchase today.'

'We could do with a new restaurant in Seacastle. Where's it going to be?' said Jasmine.

Ghita beamed and pointed through the window to the old Italian café.

'Less than a minute away,' she said, triumphant.

'Seriously? That's fantastic,' I said. 'I wonder if they want to sell me the nineteen-fifties fixtures and fittings. I've had my eye on those for almost a year.'

'I already asked for you. They say you can have them free if you clear the place out.'

I wondered how I would do that without Harry, my usual source of muscle. Hopefully, we would be on speaking terms by then.

I gave Ghita a hug.

'Thank you, angel. I'll organise it as soon as I can. Do you want a cup of tea?'

'Ooh, yes please, I'm gasping. And I think I'll have a piece of my cake.'

Five minutes later, when Ghita and Jasmine were discussing recipes for samosas, I slipped off to make a call.

'Hi.'

'Hello, are you still annoyed with me?' I said.

'I was never annoyed with you. I was annoyed with me.'

'Can we talk? I think it's time you told me about the army.'

'I can't tell you everything, but...' He sighed. 'I can tell you about my brother, Nick.'

'Your brother? I thought, I mean, I didn't know you had one.'

'I don't, anymore, not really, but Rivers has been in touch with him. That's why I got so furious. It's not his fault. He didn't realise the extent of our split.'

'So that's why you are annoyed about Helen and me?'

'I'm sorry. I'm sure it seems important to you, but you're making a mountain out of a molehill and I got frustrated. Helen loves you, in her own way, and you love her. That's a pretty good start. One I don't have.'

His voice croaked with emotion and I felt my heart tighten with sympathy.

'I'm sorry. Will you come and have supper with me and Mouse tonight? We miss you.'

'I can't come tonight, but I promise to come soon. And I think we've got some new clearances on the horizon.'

'That's okay. I managed to get some newspaper work today, so I'm going to be pretty busy. Just call me when you're in town.'

'Okay. Thanks partner. We also have a pending matter I'm all too aware of. I've been avoiding you, because of it. I don't know how to talk about it.'

'Give it time. There's no hurry. I'm not going anywhere.'

'Not even with George?'

'Especially not with him.'

After I rang off, I pondered our problem. My ex-husband George had recently had a change of heart about divorcing me. He wasn't the sort of man who gave up easily. I didn't fancy being without Harry's comforting presence at the Grotty Hovel, while George still entertained ideas about getting back together. I put my phone into my pocket and returned to the table where the women had been joined by Roz Murray, my other best friend, who had dyed her hair bright pink. I gave her a hug and sat down letting the wave of laughter and gossip roll over me. Everything would work out in the end. It always does.

Chapter 4

The Pavilion Theatre sat in domed grandeur at the entrance to Seacastle Pier. It had been rebuilt in the 1920s after the original theatre burned down. The architects were inspired by the concert halls of Rome, Nice, Vienna and Paris. The theatre specialised in summer shows with popular entertainers of the day like Rex London, and Elsie and Doris Waters. During the second world war the Pavilion was closed but used as a garrison theatre by the troops. After a refurbishment in the late seventies, the theatre went back to featuring musicals, concerts and plays. I had been taken to the theatre as a girl, although I couldn't remember what I had seen or who starred in the production.

Mouse stared up at the dome.

'It's bigger than I remember,' he said. 'I haven't really looked at it before.'

'Have you ever been to the theatre?' I said.

He snorted.

'Can you imagine George taking me to a concert, or a play?'

'He didn't take me either.'

I made a mental note to book a musical in London one weekend. Maybe we could even drag Harry there with us? We tried the front doors leading to the lobby, but they were all locked. I hadn't anticipated that. How would we get in if no one expected us? Mouse shouted that he had found the stage door and I made my way over feeling uncertain of our welcome. Maybe Jasmine had already informed the manager about me? I knocked, timidly at first, and then harder. In the distance I could hear someone saying 'all right, keep your wig on', and the sound of shuffling feet.

I heard someone jiggling a key in an old-fashioned lock and a bolt being slid back. The door swung open and a tiny, plump woman in a tweed skirt and a frilly white blouse stood in the passage way, blinking at the sudden increase in light.

'Who are you?' she said.

'Press,' I said.

'Where's your card?'

'I'm not exactly official.'

'Go away then,' said the woman, trying to shut the door.

I put my foot in the way.

'Jasmine Smith sent me. My name is Tanya Bowe. I'm—'

'Tanya Bowe? From *Uncovering the Truth*?'

'Yes, that's me. I used to do the research for the programme.'

'Oh, I know all about it. I'm such a fan. I don't know how you found out all that stuff.'

'I had to break a few rules.'

'I bet you did. Come in, and who's this?'

'I'm Mouse, Tanya's…' Mouse looked at me and I nodded. 'Son, stepson.'

'Nice to meet you both. I'm Cynthia Walters. I'm the manager of the Tribute show. I look after all the acts and make sure they're happy and get what they need.'

'Can you give me the lowdown on all the contestants? I'd be very grateful for a place to start.'

'I've got basic handouts in my office upstairs. Follow me.'

We passed a dressing room door and climbed the short narrow stairway to a similarly narrow corridor with a row of doors on the right-hand side. The corridor ended in a similar staircase leading to the opposite stage door's exit which also had a dressing room beside it. A parallel staircase ran down to the storage and under-stage areas. I could see flight cases, and pieces of scenery stored without any sign of organisation in a gloomy basement. The higgledy piggledy nature of the build made clear how often the rooms had been moved and partitioned to fit into the backstage area. Cynthia's office sat in the centre of the row.

'Jasmine told us you'd be doing in depth interviews to go with her portraits.'

'That's right. I should tell you that my niece is one of the finalists. It's a coincidence, but I want to be transparent.'

'Your niece? How wonderful. It must be Olivia. Am I right?'

'Yes. How did you know?'

'She sounds like you. Posh.'

She smirked.

'I would never refer to myself like that,' I said.

'You haven't met the other finalists. She's class compared to them.'

I had all manner of protests rise up my throat, but I held my tongue. I could see Mouse also struggling to remain quiet. The door of the office opened, hitting me in the back.

'Oh, sorry love. Didn't see you there. Hey, aren't you the tiger mum from the Shanty?'

I turned around to find myself nose to nose with Lance Emerald. Mouse's face fell.

'I'm Tanya Bowe. I'm doing the cast interviews for the Tribute Show.'

'I see you brought your Mouse with you. Frank Sinatra had a Rat Pack, but a mouse will do me just fine.'

Mouse shrank away from him, difficult to do in the tight confines of the office. Cynthia inserted herself between Mouse and Lance, and handed me a sheaf of papers.

'Here you are dear. Why don't you give those a read and then contact me to organise interviews?'

'You can do me right now,' said Lance, looking at Mouse. 'I've already had my portrait done, haven't I?'

'I've got a copy here,' said Cynthia.

She turned around without moving out of the way and reached into a stack of papers. She pulled out a square, black and white photograph of Lance and gave it to me. I examined it closely. I had to hand it to Jasmine. She had captured Lance's rakish charm perfectly. He looked into the camera lens with his chin resting on his fist. A chunky ring with a large stone caught my eye.

'I got that ring from Frank Sinatra when he played the Royal Albert Hall,' said Lance. 'It's 22 carat gold and the stone's a large garnet. See?'

He thrust his hand in my face. His breath stank of cigarettes. I tried not to grimace.

'Very nice,' I said. 'At least you have something in common.'

He didn't pick up the sarcasm.

'There are differences. I still have my hair,' he said. 'Frank had to wear a rug, you know. Do you want to interview me now?'

'Give me a minute to get organised here and I'll come and find you.'

He left again, shutting the door behind him. Cynthia looked shaken.

'That man is a menace,' she said. 'Thank goodness the show will be his last hurrah.'

'Really?' I said.

'He's retiring.'

'That's a relief,' said Mouse. 'There's something about him that makes my skin crawl.'

'You're not the only one. I don't think I've heard anyone say anything nice about him the whole time I've been here,' I said. 'Anyway, I'll get it over with and give Jasmine something to publish. She has already taken his portrait, and he is still the star of the show, whether we like it or not.'

Cynthia looked as if she would say something, but a knock on the door interrupted us. I opened it to find

Reginald Dolan standing outside. I had met Reg before. He had been the Manager of the Pavilion Theatre for the last twenty years. He dressed like Hercule Poirot and had a comically pompous manner which masked a kind heart and a ruthless efficiency with budgets.

'Tanya!' he said, and gripped me by the shoulders.

He gave me the barest of pecks on each cheek, but held me at least a foot away from him. I suspected him of being slightly OCD in his habits, but I had an affection for this odd man and his quirks.

'Reg. How lovely to see you again.'

'I'm told you'll be joining us for the lead up to the Talent Competition. I hope we'll manage to get together for a gossip at some stage.'

'I'm sure we will. This is Mouse, my stepson.'

'Charmed, I'm sure. Does he act? He'd be a wonderful Mercutio.'

Mouse looked uncomfortable. He'd never suffered a deluge of theatrical people before. He'd soon get used to it.

'He's a computer wizard.'

'Are you now? I don't suppose you've got time to help me out?'

'What with?' said Mouse.

'The social media accounts. I've got a theatre to fill and there's a train strike on the day of the show. Can you help me manipulate the algorithm and get some bums on seats? I'll pay you per hour.'

'Sounds good to me.'

'Why don't you show Mouse what you need him to do?' I said. 'You could give him some logins and so forth while I interview Lance.'

'Excellent plan. Come this way, young man.'

Chapter 5

After Mouse and Reg had disappeared into the bowels of the building, Cynthia directed me to the dressing room which was beside the second stage door to the pier. I noticed a faded star peeling from the door. Apt.

'He asked for this room so he could make a quick getaway after the show,' she said, in answer to my unasked question.

I knocked at the door and heard a volley of chesty coughs followed by a hawking sound. I waited.

'Come.'

The door swung open to reveal Lance Emerald, who had removed his clothes and now stood in his greying undershorts with a tattered smoking jacket on his top half. It hung open, exhibiting his pale, scrawny chest with its sparse hairs. He had an e-cigarette dangling from his bottom lip and his hair stuck up as if he had been taking a nap. He hawked again and turned around to spit in a tissue. Revulsion swept over me, but I tried to smile.

'Mr Emerald. I see you're ready for your close up.'

'Droll Call me Lance,' he said, throwing himself on a chaise longue and patting it in invitation. 'What do you want to know?'

I did not sit. My instincts told me to stay as close to the door as possible in case of an attempted assault. I took out my pen and notebook. I had recently learned to record things on my mobile phone and I tried to press what I thought was the record button. Annoyingly, I took a photograph of the dressing table and coat hangers instead. Definitely one to delete later. I tried to remain calm, despite feeling his cynical gaze on me. I needed to take control of the interview before he made a mockery of me so I went for the jugular.

'I understand this is your last rodeo. What made you decide to retire?'

His demeanour changed. He sat up and wrapped the smoking jacket around him, tying a knot in the belt.

'Time waits for no man.'

'Seriously, that's your answer? Can't you give me more than that?'

'Look, love. This is strictly off the record, but I'm ill. Lung cancer. It's terminal. I intend to go out in a blaze of glory. But I don't want any sympathy. You're not to write about it in the interview.'

'I won't,' I said, taken aback. 'What would you like me to write about?'

'Why don't you write about my career? It might as well go on the record.'

'Okay. How did you get started?'

'I'd always been fascinated by the stage and I never achieved anything at school. So, as soon as I could I set up a double act called the Balentines with a pal of mine. I had real talent, him not so much, but we soon got gigs. We used to do Bing Crosby and Frank Sinatra impressions. We were the talk of the town. We had bookings in all the top places; Blackpool, Scarborough, Morecambe. Once we even got a booking for the London Palladium, but our partnership turned sour. We went our separate ways. I left for the continent and spent years singing in the party circuit down Monte Carlo way.'

'Monte Carlo? That's some gig.'

'Well, they weren't all five-star joints, but I got enough work to keep going. I couldn't come back to England, so I stuck it out.'

I started to ask why he couldn't come back, but he put up his hand to stall me.

'I had my reasons.'

'Did you ever get married or have children?'

'Married? No. Children? Who knows?'

'Why did you choose Frank Sinatra as your Tribute Act?'

'We have a similar vocal range and I admired his business style.'

I raised an eyebrow at this, but decided not to ask why.

'When did Frank Sinatra give you his ring?'

He smiled and the stress disappeared from his body as quickly as it had appeared.

'Pour me a whisky and I'll tell you.'

He pointed to a bottle and grubby glass balancing on a rickety table in the corner. 'All mod cons here.'

I poured him two fingers of whisky and handed him the glass. His lizard-like fingers brushed mine as he took it from me. He sniffed my hair as I drew back.

'Nice perfume. Where were we? Oh, yes, Frank.'

He took a gulp of the whisky. Some of it dribbled down his chin and he wiped it away with the smoking jacket. My revulsion increased, but I had to hear the story. It would make my article.

'Go on.'

'I had a couple of gigs in London in the 100 Club at Oxford Circus. Since I had a friend backstage at the Albert Hall, I blagged my way in to listen to Frank Sinatra's concert. After the concert, I used my charm to wait outside his dressing room, hoping to shake his hand. The security guys grabbed me and tried to carry me outside, but he noticed and called me back. By chance, he had seen me perform in the 100 Club and had been impressed. I couldn't have been prouder. He invited me into his dressing room for a drink. We even did some singing together. He corrected my phrasing on The Way You Look Tonight. And then they interrupted us and told him he had to go to some official dinner, but before he left, he took this off his finger and gave it to me. He said he had lots of rings, but only one twin. I've never been more emotional.'

Lance sat quietly turning the ring on his finger as if still in wonder at the moment.

'And then he was gone. He retired in nineteen-ninety-five and was dead by ninety-eight.'

'He had a wonderful voice,' I said. 'It's a pity his character didn't quite match up.'

'I model myself on him. If it was good enough for Frank, it is good enough for me.'

'I didn't notice the ring when I saw you sing at the Shanty. Is there any reason you have it on now?'

'My insurance company told me not to wear it out in public. It's worth a small fortune, because of who it belonged to. If I'm going to die, I want to wear it more often. After all, I can't take it with me.'

'That's quite some story,' I said. 'Who was the other half of the Balentines? Can I interview him too?'

Cynthia knocked on the door and put her head around it.

'They'll be ready for you shortly, Lance. Could you please put some clothes on? Nobody should have to see that.'

She shook her head and shut the door again. Lance cackled.

'Have you got enough for your article?' he said.

'Probably. I'll write up my notes and give you a copy to review, if that's okay. You can ask me to change stuff or fill in the gaps.'

'Perfect. I'd better get my arse up to the stage soon or Reginald will have a kitten.'

He opened the door for me, leering at me as I left. Mouse was waiting for me outside Lance's room. Lance stepped forward.

'And the faithful Mouse is standing guard. How nice.'

He stroked Mouse's cheek before I could stop him. Mouse froze and the blood drained from his face. His eyes blazed.

'Don't you ever touch me again, you old pervert!' he said.

I'd never seen him so angry. Lance smirked at him which didn't help. Mouse lunged towards Lance, but I held up my hand to hold him back. I should never have brought him with me. I put a calming hand on his arm.

'Wait for me outside.'

Mouse turned for the exit in a single movement. Lance cackled.

'Touchy, isn't he? Don't you think he should come out of the closet?'

'He isn't in one, as far as I'm aware. We're not in the last century. Mouse makes his own choices. Thanks for the interview.'

'Don't you want to watch me rehearse?'

'No, thank you. We've got to get home. It will have to be another day.'

'Here's my card,' said Lance. 'And keep the photograph. Mouse can frame it for his room.'

Chapter 6

Mouse didn't speak on the way home. I watched him chewing his cheek and grimacing. Lance Emerald had really unsettled him. Even the sight of the wind farm illuminated in the slanting rays of the sun couldn't distract him. I strolled beside him; my head full of my own issues. Lance, I didn't care about, but I loved Harry, and I had disappointed him with my idea of support for his problem. I would have to make an effort with my sister if I wanted to convince him that I appreciated my luck in life. A slightly, tricky older sister hardly counted as a burden, and we didn't need to be dragging baggage into our relationship. Adult dating is hard.

We hadn't been home long when the doorbell rang. Mouse looked at me and I shrugged my shoulders. He stood up and went to the door. He opened it and jumped backwards as a fully charged Helen Patterson lunged forward for a hug. I guess she had expected him to be me, as she pulled back with impressive agility.

'Oh, Andy, hello,' she said.

'Mouse. It's Mouse, not Andy. Only George calls me that.'

'Does he like being called George instead of Dad?' said Helen, making Mouse bristle.

'Hi Mouse,' said Olivia, pushing past her mother. 'Hi Auntie Tanya.'

'Just Tanya,' I said, and exchanged a complicit look with Mouse.

'Okay. We'll try and remember. Tanya and Mouse. I don't know why people have to go changing their names all the time. We are Helen and Olivia, and we need a cup of tea,' said Helen.

'Builder's tea, okay?' I said, although I knew she preferred Earl Grey.

I couldn't help baiting her. Helen's whole life had been planned and executed with the rigour of a military exercise and all her objectives had been achieved. She had always wanted a house in the suburbs of London with rose bushes and a garage, and a husband with a good job, and two point four children. She got all of those, having lost a child to a miscarriage. She managed to make a joke of it, ignoring the real pain she hid deep inside. But for Helen, making a fuss was taboo, an idea she inherited from our parents.

I had broken the rules by having depression and being ill instead of pulling up my socks and getting on with it. Helen disapproved of my divorce, my shop, and my former career, and now she disapproved of Mouse. I found it hard to take. But like most families, we tried to get along and find common ground. I loved her because she was my sister, even if I didn't show it often enough. I should've known she couldn't let matters go. She took a long look around the sitting room before sighing.

'Honestly, this place looks like a junk shop. I miss your old house.'

'I happen to like junk shops. Second Home pays my bills.'

'I don't suppose you had a choice, after what happened with George.'

I bit back a reply and carried in a tray from the kitchen. We all drank a fraught cup of tea, during which Olivia, noticing the atmosphere, regaled us with stories about Hunter Norman, the charismatic, ambitious, up and coming star of the show. It became obvious she had a massive crush on him. I hoped Mouse did not feel hurt, but when I glanced at him, I saw only adoration in his gaze. She might have been only three years older than him, but she lingered an entire galaxy out of his reach. I hoped she would let him down gently.

'Speaking of Hunter Norman,' I said. 'I'm conducting interviews of all the finalists for the local newspaper and social media outlets. Is there anything I should ask him about to make the interview more interesting?'

'You didn't tell me that,' said Helen. 'I hope you won't be too intrusive.'

'The idea is to ask questions and discover new angles on the contestants. The very definition of intrusive,' I said.

'I don't know why you can't do a proper job,' she said, picking at her sleeve.

Olivia scratched her head.

'I don't know if this is the sort of thing you're looking for, but Hunter and Lance Emerald are at each other's throats all the time. Perhaps you could ask Hunter about their rivalry. Old pro unwilling to relinquish spotlight to new star, that sort of thing.'

'I'm not sure that's suitable for a profile piece, but as an article about the competition, it's got legs. Thanks.'

Olivia smirked.

'Theirs is not the only rivalry you should know about,' she said. 'Cindy Gold and Tawny Redding had a cat fight the other day. They were pulling each other's hair and yelling insults.'

'What sort of thing?' I said, wondering if I could get my notebook without disturbing her flow.

'Oh, you know. Stuff about stuck on eyebrows and lip fillers. They're both completely fake. It's rumoured Cindy is sleeping with Lance or Reg Dolan.'

'I doubt she's sleeping with Reg,' said Mouse.

I grinned.

'Our Reg is not big on contact,' I said. 'He doesn't even like shaking hands, if you haven't recently washed them.'

'Sammy would give his back teeth for a chance with Cindy,' said Olivia.

'Which one's he?' said Mouse.

'He is the Freddy Mercury tribute act. The resemblance is uncanny.'

'Wasn't Freddy Indian too?' said Helen.

'A British Parsi with roots in Bombay,' I said. 'I can't wait to interview him.'

'Then there's Lance,' said Olivia. 'We all think he can't retire fast enough. He's abusive.'

'In what way?' I said, but I could imagine.

Helen stood up.

'Do you want to see our house?' she said.

'Of course,' said Mouse, taking the hint. 'I've never seen Hades's first home.'

'Hades?' said Olivia.

'Their cat,' said Helen. 'Couldn't you tell from the name?'

Hades popped in through the cat flap as if summoned by the Gods. He arched his back and stuck his tail straight into the air when he saw visitors. He walked towards us stiff legged with caution. Helen let out a mewing sound and he ran over to her and started to do a figure of eight around her ankles, purring with abandon. Soon Olivia and Helen were both stroking and whispering endearments to him as he sat between their chairs, soaking up the adoration. I sat watching, stewing with jealousy. Mouse gave me a sympathetic smile.

'Right. That's enough cat spoiling. I thought you were going to show me your house,' I said. 'I'm dying of curiosity.'

'Come on then,' said Helen, heading for the door.

'Be careful not to let Hades out onto the street. He's not used to traffic,' said Mouse.

'But how will he visit us?' said Olivia.

'The back garden fence between the two houses has a loose plank in it. I can remove it while you are here so he has a safe route next door,' said Mouse.

'Oh, would you?' said Olivia, fluttering her eyelashes and making him blush.

Poor lad. He had been lonely since Amanda left, but Olivia Patterson did not seem to be the solution. She had a crush on someone else, and she struck me as a taker, not a giver. Mind you, I didn't know her well. I hadn't seen much of Helen or her family for years due to my illness.

Next door's front entrance had been recently painted and the new lock resisted Helen's attempts to force it open. Mouse took the key and twisted it with gentle persuasion until the levers sprung. Helen thanked him with bad grace. We pushed our way through the front door into a pristine world of beechwood fittings, magnolia walls and the entirety of the IKEA catalogue. I struggled to recall the dingy, abandoned property where I had met Harry, and rescued Hades and his laundry basket. The new owners had removed all character from the house. The rooms were the same size as mine, but they did not resemble my vintage-explosion decorative style in any way.

'This is nice,' I said. 'All mod cons.'

'It's gorgeous, isn't it. I wish I could redo my house like this,' said Helen.

I stifled a snort. Helen's house wallowed in Laura Ashley prints and plump cushions on pastel carpets. I found it hard to imagine her swapping it for Swedish hard edges and primary colours. I looked around, taking in the 'improvements'. The Victorian fireplace had been removed and the hole bricked up. In its place an enormous flat-screen television was attached to the wall. Mouse yelped in delight when he found a popcorn maker in the alcove beside it.

'Who's up for movie night?' he said.

'We'll be much too busy,' said Helen. 'Olivia has to practice for the competition.'

'And give me an interview,' I said.

'You're going to interview me?' said Olivia. 'What fun!'

'And Jasmine will come and take a portrait of you too.'

'As I said. We won't have a minute before the competition for socialising,' said Helen. 'I'm sure Mouse is far too busy hanging out with his friends to bother with us.'

Mouse's face fell. He's not much good with social signals, but he received the snub loud and clear. I rolled my eyes at him, but he ignored me.

'I need to practice my songs,' said Olivia.

'You can sing for me if you like,' he said. 'I'd love to hear your songs.'

'Really? I'd like that. I'll bring my guitar over later.'

'Great. Everyone's happy then. Thank you for the tips, Olivia. I'm going to write them down before I forget.'

Olivia rubbed her chin.

'Do you know how to use the internet?' she said, as she let us out of the front door. 'Only Mum said you can't, but I don't believe that.'

'I get by. Mouse taught me,' I said, trying not to sound defensive.

'You should Google Lance Emerald. He's got a past. And he's not the only one.'

Chapter 7

The next morning, I set off along the promenade for Second Home, breathing in big lungfuls of sea air thick with the smell of rotting seaweed which made me slightly nauseous. My mind had whirred all night after the juicy titbits of gossip I had obtained from Olivia. Mouse had offered to research Lance Emerald for me as I had other obligations. Rohan and Kieron had signed the purchase agreement for the Italian café and needed me to take the furniture and fittings out immediately so the builders could move in. They were loading a furniture van at their old house in Brighton so they had left the key with Ghita who waited outside, jumping up and down with impatience like the Energiser Bunny.

'What kept you?' she said, although I arrived five minutes early.

I gave her a hug and breathed in her odour of spices and patchouli, one of my favourite hugs. Only Flo, the forensic consultant, came close when I considered my list of best huggers. And Harry, of course, but he smelled of soap and toast and rumpled beds. Maybe we should bottle people's odours and keep them so we can sniff them when we are feeling low.

'I'm expecting reinforcements,' I said. 'Mouse has asked Goose and Cracker to help us.'

'Isn't Goose the young electrician who helped us with the CCTV feed?'

'That's the one.'

'And Cracker? I don't remember him.'

'According to George, Cracker's skill set runs to safes and house breaking, but he operates around Chichester where the pickings are better.'

'Goodness, Mouse's friends certainly are an eclectic bunch, aren't they?'

'That's the polite way of putting it. Shh. Here they come.'

The two young men strolled towards us, drinking cans of Red Bull and laughing. They were both shaven headed and muscular wearing sleeveless t-shirts with faded designs. They could have been twins.

'Hi Goose. Great to see you again. And Cracker. How's it going?'

'Who's this?' said Cracker, indicating Ghita with a flick of his chin.

'I'm Ghita, Mr Cracker.'

He snorted with laughter.

'Just Cracker. Not Mr. But thanks. Miss Ghita.'

Ghita blushed prettily and he looked bashful.

'Your mission today, should you choose to accept it, is to empty this café into the antique shop over there. I will help you here, and Ghita will show you where to put things in the shop. Understood?'

'Will your message self-destruct in 5 seconds? My memory is terrible,' said Goose.

'Will coffee and a slice of chocolate cake help?' said Ghita.

'Absolutely. And I'll show Cracker the office if you don't mind. I'm proud of my work up there.'

Ghita and I swapped keys and she walked across the road to Second Home. The lock on the door of the Italian restaurant resisted me when I inserted the key and it took me a few goes to release it. Everything rusts at the seaside. I had to give the door a good shove to open it as the wood had swelled from all the rain which had been absorbed into the frame. The interior of the Italian café smelled musty when we entered, but aside from the dust on the table tops, the place appeared spotless. I pointed out the lacquered tables and chairs with their bright red tops to Goose and Cracker who began to move them out and across the street to Second Home. Their banter flowed unabated as they lifted the tables and chairs out of the door and across the street.

I could still imagine the red and white checked tablecloths and the black wire menu holders on the table when the café was open. Mr Bonetti, the owner, worked there from midday to late, six days a week and closed the café on Sundays. His wife came to help in the busy hours and his children would wait on tables at weekends. It had been the main social hub down our end of the street for thirty-five years and I identified it with some of the best moments of my younger life. When the Bonettis announced they were going home to Italy, a whole generation of Seacastle residents mourned their decision. They had looked for someone to take it on, but nobody wanted to manage a café down the cheap end of Seacastle.

Now that Rohan and Kieron had taken it over, the wisdom of opening a high-end Indian fusion restaurant in our end of town seemed flawed, but I kept my opinion to myself. The Italian café had always been full because of the atmosphere, the food and the great coffee. Rohan and Kieron had the right characters to replace the Bonettis with a new vibrant version. And then there were Ghita's recipes. Not many people would resist the temptation to come again after they had tried her dishes once.

I pointed out several light fittings to the boys which I could sell in the shop, as well as the curvy front desk with a fat red lip around top edge. As the place emptied, I brushed the floor from back to front, pushing the pile towards the doorway. Cracker walked right through it, scattering the dust again, but I didn't say anything, just gathered the dust with my broom. He walked straight through it again, and then they both burst out laughing. I rolled my eyes.

'Hilarious. Take those last things across the road and get Ghita to make you a coffee. I'll be right there.'

Mr Bonetti had decorated the walls with pictures of local celebrities, but now squares of cleaner paint marked their absence, making me feel sad. The pile of photographs in black and red photograph frames sat on the counter where the young men had placed them. I shuffled through them, recognising some minor stars who had disappeared from public view and felt a little sad for them. The names would not come to me. Two of the frames were already empty, but I removed the remaining photographs and put them in a large envelope I found under the desk. Then I took the stack of frames and the envelope across the road to Second Home. Ghita took them from me and I returned to lock up the café. I took one final look at the now barren interior, stripped of all my memories, and locked the door. I had to remind myself that time moves on, and change is good.

I found Ghita upstairs in the Vintage with the boys looking at the photographs which they had removed from the envelope.

'Wow, those hippy hairstyles are rad,' said Goose, rubbing his hand over his hair. 'I don't think my girlfriend would approve tho.'

Cracker sneered.

'They're probably all dead by now.'

Goose laughed.

'You're just jealous. Cos you're already going bald.'

Cracker punched his arm.

'Get lost. They're all batty boys. Give me my money. I'm out of here.'

He held out his hand and sweat stood out on his brow. I nodded.

'Of course. You don't want to hang around with us all day. Come downstairs and I'll get it out of the register.'

I had forgotten we had not sold anything, and the register drawer opened with a hollow sound.

'Oops. Never mind, I'll get my handbag.'

I retrieved it from behind the counter and removed my copy of the local newspaper to find my wallet. The front page featured my article about Lance Emerald and Cracker rolled his eyes.

'I can't escape from that bastard,' he said. 'He's everywhere.'

He picked up the paper and folded it. I realised he wanted it, although I couldn't fathom why.

'Take it if you want. I've already read it.'

'It's not for me. My mum loves him. Silly cow.'

'Do I know her?'

'Probably. Everyone does.'

Before I could ask him her name, he grabbed the money and the newspaper and left. Goose, who had come downstairs, shrugged at me.

'I don't know what's got into him. He can be a little volatile. Thanks for the money.'

'What's Cracker's real name?'

'I don't know. Nobody does.'

He smiled and followed Cracker outside. I returned upstairs and Ghita handed me the photos. I gazed at them conjuring up the old seaside entertainments of my parents' era. I would have liked to put the names to the faces, but, for now, they were a mystery.

'What was that all about?' said Ghita.

'I don't know. I think Cracker's a troubled lad. He's nice most of the time, but Mouse says he can be unpredictable. And George has his eye on him for a couple of burglaries.'

'Ah, well, the good thing is, he won't be back here.'

'And how do you know that?'

'There's no money in the till.'

"That reminds me. Help me put the Edwardian dresser in the window. We can make bets on how long it will take Grace to spot it.'

'Is she so predictable?'

'I know her taste. And she can double the amount if she sells it in her shop.'

'No wonder she wants to steal Harry.'

'Not a chance.'

Chapter 8

I left Roz in charge of the shop the next day, to devote the time to catching up on my interviews. I wanted to quiz Lance on his start in show business, so I could include more about it in my general piece about the show. All the contestants were due at the theatre to prepare for dress rehearsals. Mouse came with me to film TikToks and video clips to be used for publicity. Reg Dolan had been thrilled when he discovered the extent of Mouse's social media savvy.

'Honestly, darling. I haven't a clue. It would be good if we could drum up some excitement in Seacastle. We're not exactly on the beaten track here, and the rail strike threatened for show day is not going to help. I have to persuade the locals to buy tickets or the theatre could be half empty.'

We walked along the promenade past the Mr Whippy van which had not yet started up. The man who ran it scrubbed the paintwork until the garish colours gleamed wet in the morning sunlight.

'Can we have one later?' said Mouse. 'I'd really like to eat a ninety-nine and sit in the wind shelter looking at the sea.'

I examined him, trying to decipher his mood,

'Are you okay?' I said. 'You can tell me, whatever it is.'

He shook his head.

'I'm fine. I just feel like eating an ice cream.'

We knocked on the stage door which was opened by someone who looked so like Freddy Mercury, including the massive overbite, that I let out a yelp. Sammy Singh grinned at me.

'The resemblance is remarkable, I know. It's a pity my voice isn't, but you can't have everything. Are you Tanya Bowe? I've heard you'll be doing the interviews with us.'

'That's right. And this is Mouse, my stepson.'

'Ah, the great Hackini. I've heard of you too.'

He tapped the side of his nose and Mouse avoided his look of complicity.

'Hackini?' I said, raising an eyebrow.

'It's a joke,' said Mouse. 'Nobody calls me that. Anyway, I wouldn't. George is just waiting for the chance to chase me out of the Grotty Hovel.'

'George is history,' I said, and turned back to Sammy. 'Do you know where I can find Lance Emerald?'

'He's in the leading man's dressing room, of course. I don't think Hunter is overjoyed to be sharing with us plebs.'

'It's the last time. Then you can compete with Hunter in a dance off for top billing.'

'Now that's one competition I'd win. Hunter has two left feet. Or three.'

He barked out a laugh. I got the feeling there was no love lost between the two young men. He directed us through the labyrinth of narrow passageways to a door with a single star it.

'Voila!'

'Thank you. I've just got to ask him one question and I'll come and interview you, if that's okay?'

'Not really. I'm due on stage soon. Can't we do this immediately?'

I hesitated, but his impatience persuaded me. I didn't want to irritate him before our interview. Sammy Singh turned out to be charming and determined in equal measure. He had a disarming way about him, but I suspected it hid a core of steel. I longed to ask him if he ever got teased about his teeth, and whether it drove him on, but it didn't seem fair. The version of his life that he fed me felt sanitised somehow, but there appeared little doubt that his startling resemblance to Freddy Mercury had smoothed his path. He had cultivated that shy goofiness I had seen in documentaries about Freddy. Honestly, it was as if the real version had been cloned.

'When did you know you were bound for show business?' I asked him.

'When I failed my practical exam at A-Level Chemistry and I had no hope of going to university to be a doctor. My parents were disappointed, but not surprised. I knew more than most people about the career, since they were both doctors, but I just couldn't get enthusiastic about anything except singing and dancing.'

'Plus, you had a made to measure tribute act waiting.'

'I inhabit the man when I'm on stage. We are so similar, in every way. It was a no-brainer as far as I'm concerned.'

We spent a pleasant half an hour together after our interview veered into the realm of collecting antiques. His eyes lit up when I told him about the glass fisherman's floats that I sold at Second Home. He promised to come by the shop and have a tea in the window to startle the passersby and hopefully increase footfall. In return, I offered him his choice of Ghita's wonderful cakes and a tour of the shop, including the storeroom at the back. He offered me a signed copy of his publicity shot 'to hang in the shop'. I took it out of politeness. I couldn't imagine it looking anything except out of place there, but it reminded me I should do something with the vintage photos from the Italian café. Maybe reframe them in a collage for the Vintage.

'I'd better get ready for my rehearsal,' he said, finally.

'Is it true you and Hunter don't get on,' I said, on a whim.

He went rigid and turned to me, his face dark with fury.

'And who told you that?'

'I don't remember. Were they mistaken?'

He sneered.

'We're not bosom buddies, if that's what you're asking. This competition could make us or break us. We're rivals. Machiavelli rules around here.'

'The end justifies the means?'

'Exactly.'

'Break a leg,' I said, standing up to tidy my stuff into my handbag.

'I might, if Hunter has anything to do with it.'

Suddenly, Mouse burst in, his eyes wide.

'You're here. Thank goodness. Something terrible has happened. It's Lance Emerald.'

'What on earth's he done now?' I said, mildly exasperated and imagining all sorts of misdemeanours.

'He's dead. Someone strangled him in his dressing room. It's horrible. You must come now.'

'Have you called the police?' said Sammy.

'George has just arrived,' said Mouse. 'The D.I. He's my Dad.'

'Your father's the Detective Inspector? Now that's weird,' said Sammy.

I noticed that the concept of someone strangling Lance didn't strike him as weird or even horrific. He took the news with as much interest as if someone had burnt the toast.

'You don't seem too shocked,' I said.

'I doubt they'll find anyone who didn't want that weasel dead. I'm sorry, but good riddance to bad rubbish.'

I couldn't think of a reply. Mouse tugged my arm, and I followed him out of the room. Sammy's reaction had been so low key that I felt as if the so-called murder was a prank and Lance would be in his room leering at me and sipping his whisky, and not dead after all. We hurried along the corridor and to the stairs, back to the dressing room where I had interviewed Lance. Then I spotted Olivia coming up the stairs from the basement. She appeared dishevelled and distressed. I yelled a greeting, but she didn't stop. I heard a door slam, but I couldn't tell which one. There wasn't time to find out, with Lance lying dead.

My ex-husband, D.I. George Carter, stood guard over the doorway, shielding the room from new finger prints or other contaminants of the forensic evidence. A small group had gathered on the stairs, conversing in aptly named stage whispers. I recognised Cindy and someone I took to be Tawny talking to Cynthia and Reg. Hunter appeared panting from upstairs.

'What's up?' he said.

'He's dead,' said Cindy. 'Honest, he's in there. I saw him with my own eyes.'

'How did he die?' said Tawny. 'I hope it was painful.'

'There's no need for that,' said Cynthia. 'You shouldn't speak ill of the dead, no matter what you think.'

'He had it coming,' said Hunter. 'About time too.'

'Did you do it?' said Cindy. 'You're the one who benefits most.'

'No, but I can't say it's a tragedy. I don't know many people here who like the man.'

'That's enough,' said Reg. 'I need you to clear off now and sit in your rooms. Doubtless, the police will be around soon to take your statements.'

'But I had a date,' said Tawny.

'And now you don't,' said Cynthia. 'Cancel it.'

I pushed my way through them, muttering that I had to speak to D.I. Carter. Mouse followed behind, clinging onto the strap of my handbag, his gaze on the floor.

I arrived at George's side and peered into the room. The shocking sight of Lance Emerald lying on the chaise longue with a Seagulls' scarf tied around his neck met my gaze. The sky-blue colour matched his alarmingly blue face, a strange combination he might have appreciated had he been alive to see it. Mouse had a haunted look which struck me as odd.

'Did you find the body?' said George.

Mouse nodded, unable to articulate his thoughts. George eyed us with suspicion.

'I should've known you two would be involved,' he said. 'What are you doing here?'

'We're working. Is it against the law now?'

He shrugged.

'Do you know anything about this guy,' he said, gesticulating at Lance.

'I did an interview with him a couple of days ago. And I came to see him earlier, but Sammy Singh needed me to do his interview first, so I didn't go in.'

George rolled his eyes.

'Better and better,' he said. 'Now you might be the last person to see him alive.'

'I told you I didn't enter the room. And I didn't kill him if that's what you're insinuating. From what I hear, I would have had to join the queue if I wanted to murder him.'

'Popular guy, huh? Well, Flo should be here with the forensic technician any minute. Maybe she'll tell me he killed himself by mistake. Overtightened his scarf, perhaps?'

'He's dead. Do you have to make a joke about everything?' said Mouse.

'Weren't you the one who found him, Andy? I'd watch my tongue if I were you.'

Mouse's real name jarred with me as it always did. I knew Mouse hated being called Andy. Only George and

Helen still persisted, as everybody knew he preferred to be called Mouse. Mouse glared at George and seemed to be about to say something, but the remainder of the group parted like the Red Sea as the formidable galleon that was Flo Barrington, the consultant pathologist, sailed through followed by her lanky assistant, Joseph. He always reminded me of Beaker on the Muppet show with his stiff, uncombed, red locks. Flo gave me a brief hug before her ample frame, topped with a chaotic bun of grey-streaked black hair, filled the small dressing room. She went about her duties making notes on her iPad and tutting as Joseph tried to stay out of her way and help at the same time.

'Shine that light in his face,' she said, leaning over and examining Lance's face with a magnifying glass.

Joseph twisted the arc light so it lit Lance's swollen face. It looked like a prop from a horror movie. Flo pulled out an old-fashioned magnifying glass and leaned in to examine his face. A drop of sweat rolled down her brow as the exertion told on her knees. After examining his face and neck with exaggerated care, she grunted and levered herself upright by pushing on her thigh. She made another note in her iPad and turned to George.

'Definitely strangled,' she said. 'Petechial haemorrhaging in the eyes and facial congestion. I'll have another look in the autopsy, but I'd say death by strangulation within the last hour. It's tropical in here, so the body temperature hasn't cooled much since he died. I can't be sure of the time of death until I have a closer look at the evidence.'

She bent over and carefully removed the scarf and dropped it into an evidence bag produced and held open by Joseph. Then she took the sealed bag and examined the scarf closely.

'It's got some writing on the label,' she said, and peered through the plastic with her magnifying glass. Then she turned and I saw the look of distress on her face before she spoke.

'The writing on the label says Mouse.'

Mouse's mouth dropped open. I murmured in shock.

'My scarf?' said Mouse. 'But I haven't seen it for months. I bought a replacement. You can ask Tanya.'

'He did. It's hanging on the coat rack at home,' I said. 'I don't understand.'

George looked at Mouse in disbelief for a second, but then his hard professional exterior recrystallised.

'You both need to come down to the station with me and give statements,' he said. 'As the last people to see Lance Emerald alive, you may have important information for the enquiry. We'll sort out the scarf thing later.'

'But we didn't go in. He may have been dead already.'

'So you say.'

P.C. Brennan had arrived at George's side and stood. George patted him on the shoulder.

'You need to cordon off the corridor and interview everyone in the theatre. Give the station a call and ask if anyone can help you. See if you can lay your hands on a key for the dressing room. We must keep people away until forensics have had a thorough search. Have you finished with the victim, Flo?'

'For now. He smells of drink. Make sure they test the bottle for fingerprints.'

I sighed and George raised an eyebrow.

'What now?'

'I poured him a drink. During the interview I did with him two days ago. My prints will be on the bottle and maybe still on the glass.'

George swore under his breath.

'What a train wreck! I can't interview my ex-wife and my son about a murder. I'll have to get in a neutral party from the Brighton station. Maybe D.I. Antrim can take over.'

'It's not our fault,' said Mouse. 'Nobody liked him. Anybody could have done it.'

'But you two are the short odds favourites right now,' said George. 'Come on. I'll take you down to the station.'

Chapter 9

Mouse and I sat in the waiting room at the station for hours waiting for the visiting D.I. to interview us. We both read every leaflet and examined every mugshot before running out of things to do. From his reaction to one of the them, Mouse had more than a passing acquaintance with one of the young men pictured. I saw him stifle a smirk as he read the charges, but I decided not to say anything. Sally Right, the receptionist, also acted as a listening post for the station and had been known to pick up private conversations with her sticking out ears. She took pity on us after Mouse's stomach made itself heard, and brought us sandwiches and teas from the canteen.

'We can't have you starving in the station. It wouldn't look good,' she said.

'I never thanked you for your help with Roz,' I said. 'She is so grateful.'

She snorted.

'So grateful that she hasn't found time to thank me?'

'You know Roz. Always rushing somewhere on her bike. I expect she'll get around to it eventually.'

Unlikely, but I didn't want to admit it. As I sipped my tea and Mouse scrolled manically on his phone, the door of the station opened and PC Brennan came in. He couldn't look me in the eye.

'Hello,' I said.

'I need you both to come with me, so I can take your fingerprints,' he said, looking at the floor. 'It's for elimination purposes, you know, at the crime scene.'

'Okay,' I said, pulling Mouse's arm.

P.C. Brennan showed us into the fingerprinting suite and put our finger and palm prints into the system using the Livescan. Mouse, who is the biggest geek on the planet, got quite emotional with excitement. His enthusiasm caused P.C. Brennan to relax and soon they were discussing how the machine worked and what the Scene Examiner would do to eliminate our prints from the enquiry.

Suddenly the door of the suite opened and a tall gaunt man, his hair stuck to his head with Brilliantine, stalked in. I recognised him as D.I. Terry Antrim, the scourge of the south coast, as he was known. George had had several run-ins with him in the past. I could imagine his glee at having George's ex-wife and son at his mercy. He wore a sardonic smile as he approached.

'I hear you're both in the frame for the murder at the Pavilion. Which one of you wants to give me your version of events first? How about you, Mrs Carter?'

He waved a bony finger in my face.

'My name is Bowe. And I'm not Mrs anything, but I can help your enquiry if you wish.'

'Come with me, Ms Hoity Toity, and drop the attitude. Your fingerprints are all over the murder scene from what I hear, so I'd be a little more polite, if I were you.'

'Tanya had nothing to do with it,' said Mouse.

'Ah, the spawn of Satan. I'd mind my Ps and Qs too if you know what's good for you. Take him back outside to the waiting area, P.C. Brennan.'

Mouse looked as if he might reply, but I held a finger up to my lips and mouthed 'leave it' at him. He frowned and went into a sulk, stabbing his fingers at his mobile phone keyboard. I got up and followed the skeletal frame of D.I. Antrim through the security doors into the station.

As usual, I got some sly looks and half waves from George's team, most of whom had known me for years as his long-suffering wife. We entered the meeting room with the metal table and nylon carpet and I steeled myself for an electric shock. I collect electricity like a battery and then give myself a shock every time I touch metal after walking on polyester carpets. When I was married to George, I used to make him open the car door for me in the winter, so I could avoid giving myself what felt like electric shock treatment every time I got into my car. I tried to pull the chair out with my shoe to avoid touching it.

'Afraid of germs, Ms Bowe? There will be more variety in the cell tonight.'

I didn't take the bait. I knew enough about policing to know that he had, so far anyway, no evidence to tie me to the crime. In a way, I wished it had been my scarf. The presence of Mouse's scarf around Lance's scrawny chicken neck had shaken me to the core, although I hid it well. How on earth had it got there? Was someone trying to frame Mouse? I would never have believed Mouse capable of such a thing, despite his fury and impotence when faced with Lance's predatory advances.

'No, just electric shocks.'

'Take your shoes off. That works. It earths you.'

I slipped off my trainers and was embarrassed to find my socks were emitting an unpleasant pong. Too late I noticed Antrim's nostrils flare. He smirked.

'Are you trying to poison me too?' he said.

'Hilarious.'

I pulled out my chair and still got a shock. I swore and shook my arm.

'Bummer,' he said. 'Let's get down to business.'

He turned on the recording equipment and stated the time and date and the names of the people in the room. Then he fixed me with his piercing grey eyes and drummed his fingers on the table. I waited. I recognised the trick. George had told me all about interrogating suspects while we were married. He liked to show off about his technique. I sat back in my chair and breathed out slowly through my mouth, trying to release all the tension. My shoulders sank and I allowed myself a smile. I could see how much it riled him. I should have told Mouse about all this stuff, but I never imagined we would be suspects in a murder inquiry. I considered writing him a note to slip him as we swapped places, but I knew I wouldn't get away with it.

'Why were you at the theatre today?'

I blinked several times as I brought myself back to the table.

'Sorry?'

'The theatre? What were you doing there?'

'Oh, yes, of course. I took a gig writing profiles of the competitors in the National Tribute Show. I intended to interview several of the performers today.'

'And Andy?'

'Who?'

Andy, Your stepson?'

'Oh, he's called Mouse. No one calls him Andy, except George, and my sister Helen, and it really annoys him.'

'Does it now?' he said, making a note on his phone with a stylus.

Damn.

'What was Mouse doing at the theatre?'

'Reg Dolan, the manager of the theatre is a bit of a Luddite and he wanted Mouse to help him with the social media announcements for the competition. Mouse is a genius with the internet and that kind of stuff.'

'Like all boys his age,' said Antrim. 'I've got one of those.'

He almost relaxed for an instant, but then his eyes turned cold again.

'Tell me about the interview with Lance.'

'Two days ago, I interviewed Lance in the same dressing room where Mouse found him strangled. I asked him questions about his career and he told me about his start in show business and his meeting with Frank Sinatra.'

'Have you met Lance before?'

'Yes, once. He did a gig at the Shanty pub not so long ago.'

'Did you get on well with him? Rumour has it he united people in their dislike of him.'

'He was a complete scumbag, but he had a beautiful voice.'

'Did he make a pass at you?'

'Absolutely not. He had a preference for young people.'

'Like Mouse?'

His keen gaze seemed to scald me as he waited for an answer. I swallowed.

'He expressed an interest, but Mouse found him repulsive.'

'Mouse's scarf is likely to be the murder weapon. Do you think Mouse lost his temper and strangled Lance?'

'No. We haven't seen that scarf for months. I'm not sure when it went missing. Maybe someone is trying to frame Mouse for murder?'

'That's a possibility. Does anyone have a grudge against Mouse?'

'Not that I know of. He's popular and kind hearted. I don't know anyone who doesn't like him.'

I crossed my fingers under the table. His father didn't like him, but I was pretty sure George didn't kill Lance.

'We needed to take your fingerprints to eliminate them from the enquiry.'

'I knew that.'

Or to prove I saw Lance just before he died…

'That's all for now. Mouse is technically an adult so I will interview him alone. Any objections?'

'No. You'll find him articulate and intelligent. There's no way he killed Lance. He found himself in the wrong place at the wrong time.'

'Unlike me. This is my chance to get replace George in this cushy job. He's past his prime, and you two just gave me the perfect opening to prove my worth.'

My mouth fell open. I couldn't believe what I was hearing.

'Don't act so surprised,' he said. 'Anyway, he's your ex. What do you care?'

As I made my way back to the waiting room, I wished I had time to brief Mouse on D.I. Antrim's technique. I trusted Mouse but he could be a little hot-headed if riled. I hoped he didn't attract attention to himself with incendiary answers. Mouse squeezed my hand before he followed D.I. Antrim through the secure door. It made me feel better for less than a minute. I fretted and panicked for what seemed like hours until he came back through the door. I had tried to distract myself by making a list of the suspects. I discounted Sammy, because I had been interviewing him around the time of the murder. Everyone else in the theatre had access to the dressing room and the possibility of slipping in and out of it without anyone noticing. As usual, I needed to find out who had a motive. D.I. Antrim had an axe to grind against George and I wanted to thwart him by solving the case before he did, handing the murderer to George on a plate. I didn't like the way Antrim looked at me. Not one bit.

Mouse finally emerged pale and shaken. D.I. Antrim approached me.

'I'm letting him go home, but only if you'll vouch for him. He's a prime suspect right now.'

'You have my word.'

'And don't interfere with my case. We've heard about you and your posse, up in Brighton. I'm not like George. I won't tolerate it, if you get in my way.'

I nodded and put my arm around Mouse's shoulder. D.I. Antrim watched us as we left the station, practically holding each other up. Mouse let out a long breath as we stepped outside.

'Are you okay,' I said. 'D.I. Antrim is a beast.'

'He practically accused me of murdering Lance. You believe I didn't do it, don't you?'

'Of course I do. We need to find out who did it, though. That man is gunning for George's position. He told me he intended to force George to retire early. Let's go home. And we still need a Mr Whippy.'

Chapter 10

The next morning, I left a mildly traumatised Mouse to sleep in. We had endured a visit from Helen and Olivia the night before, who were both agog at our ordeal in the interview room. Olivia examined Mouse's hands for ink from the fingerprinting, and had been disappointed to hear about the Livescan machine. I noticed spots of colour appear in Mouse's cheeks when she held his hands. I wondered how her crush on Hunter had progressed. I hadn't managed to interview him yet, but he didn't strike me as someone I'd fancy going out with.

Helen did not waste any sympathy on us.

'It's not like either of you killed him, is it? Good riddance to bad rubbish as far as I'm concerned.'

'That's way harsh,' said Mouse.

'The man had terminal cancer,' I said. 'A little sympathy would be nice.'

'Olivia tells me he had no redeeming characteristics. There's no point in mourning a man like that.'

As usual, Helen's judgement on the matter did not take any shade of grey into account. Her world only had two colours, black and white. Perhaps Harry would be more understanding of my difficulties with Helen if he actually met her? I made a mental note to organise it. She still thought I should go back to George, so I doubted Harry would meet with her approval. It would be interesting to put them in the same room.

Roz had left me a note under the counter in Second Home, wrapped around a bundle of ten-pound notes. I knew before I had read it, that Grace had dropped in and bought the dresser. She only dealt in cash as far as I could make out. Max and Grace liquidated their assets when they left Hong Kong, and their close shave had resulted in them hoarding cash, just in case. Or as Grace always called it, 'you never know' money. The note read: 'You won the bet. I owe you a latte. BTW, I heard about the murder. You're turning into Jessica Fletcher'.

I grinned. JF, from the TV series *Murder She Wrote,* would have felt right at home in Seacastle. It had certain similarities to Cabot Cove, one of them being the Sheriff. I had heard whispers about George and his tendency to pick the criminal before getting the evidence, but it never occurred to me they might be true. The George that I knew had often relied on my advice to get to the truth, but why not use an asset if you had it at hand?

The doorbell clanged and I looked up to see him standing in front of me, as if summoned by my thought waves. George did not look well. I hadn't noticed in the gloom of the theatre corridor, but he had gained more weight and he needed a haircut. His shirt looked as if it had been bundled up when wet and dried like that without ironing. I wasn't much of a wife, for various reasons, not all my fault, but I used to enjoy ironing his shirts for work in front of my favourite cozy mystery series on the tv in the afternoon. I found it soothing.

'Hello,' he said. 'Are you busy?'

We both looked around the shop which ached with emptiness and smirked at each other.

'Nothing I can't do later,' I said. 'Do you fancy a coffee and a stick of celery?'

'Yes, please. I hope that's code for cake. Sharon has still got me on this diet. I think it makes me eat more instead of less.'

I twisted the sign in the door to closed and released the lock. We climbed the stairs and George sat on the banquette. I headed for the coffee machine to load up the portafilter and placed two cups under the nozzles.

'Latte? You can cut yourself a piece of cake. This week's special is orange and lemon, or there's some left-over chocolate sponge.'

'I'd better have an Americano if I'm having cake. I think I'll have a sliver of each.'

'Good choice. Ghita's cakes are dangerously delicious.'

I brought us over the coffees and George took a mouthful of the orange and lemon cake. He shut his eyes as it hit his tongue.

'Damn the diet.'

'Hmm. Did you come here only to eat cake? Or to see me too?'

He began to reply, but a crumb went down the wrong way and he started to cough. I thumped him on the back harder than I needed to, irritated at him for no reason other than the usual resentment at being dumped. He went bright red in the face before he could control his coughing, and then looked miserable, all podgy and pink and lost.

'Honestly, you look like an orphaned piglet. What on earth is wrong with you?'

'Oh, that's right. Kick a man when he's down. I deserve it.'

'Sorry, that was uncalled for. Tell me.'

'It's Antrim. He's after my job.'

'He told me.'

'He told you? What a cheek that man has! He's been waiting for his chance to show me up ever since he arrived in Brighton.'

'And now he has it. I'm sorry. It feels like my fault.'

'It's a horrible coincidence, but you can help me beat him at his own game.'

'What do you need?'

'I'm not allowed to investigate the murder while you and Mouse are suspects. I need you to use your access to find out who had motive and opportunity to kill Lance Emerald. Once you are exonerated, I'll be able to run with the information and beat him to the murderer.'

'And what about Mouse? His scarf is the murder weapon, and Lance harassed him. He also found the body. Some people might call that motive and means.'

'My Andy couldn't harm a fly. He's just not capable. Do you know how long it takes to strangle someone?'

I laughed.

'He'd get bored and look at his mobile phone instead.'

George guffawed.

'Look. I'm sorry I put you under pressure, about getting back together. It took me a long time to admit to myself that I made a mistake. I know you are interested in Harry, and there's nothing I can do about that, but I'd like you to give me a chance to prove I'm serious.'

'And Sharon?'

He sighed.

'I won't leave her if you don't want me back. I'm not the sort of man who can cope by himself.'

That rang true, but as much as I disliked Sharon, I couldn't let him woo me and live with her at the same time.

'You know I can't agree to that. Sharon may not be my favourite person, but you need to be free to court me. I won't play your game this time. However, I will help you with the case. I don't like Antrim and he doesn't like me. I'll consider it a challenge to send him back to Brighton with his tail between his legs. Will that do for the time being?'

'It's a deal. Can I have some more cake?'

'You mean you want to have your cake and eat it too?'

'Shut up and cut me a slice of that orange and lemon one.'

Chapter 11

After George had gone, I reopened the shop, but the only customers were some day trippers who had nothing better to do. At least they had a pot of tea. The last of the big spenders. While they had a natter upstairs, I dug out some nice photograph frames I had bought at the car boot sale. One of them had room for three photographs and another for a pair of portraits. I also had a Victorian silver frame which had languished in the glass display case on my counter top for months.

I took out the envelope of photographs I had rescued from the Italian café and I laid them out on a small table downstairs. I shuffled them several times. The photographs fell into two groups; the singers and the dancers. By chance, three were of singers and four of dancing troupes. The dancing troupes were composed of women in sequined outfits decorated with feathers and looked as if they might be slightly risqué acts. The three men were wearing tails and in full voice. They looked like penguins with their beaks open. It occurred to me that the photographs might be useful prompts when interviewing people at the theatre for the general article. I used the camera on my phone to record them individually and copy them all into a folder marked Pavilion theatre.

The photographs fitted into the larger frames after I trimmed them slightly at the sides. I tried not to cut away any important period details before inserting the photographs into the frames. I hung them in a prominent place on the wall downstairs, and put the silver frame into the glass display. As I admired my handiwork, my mobile phone rang. Flo! Excellent.

'It's me. Are you busy tonight?'

'Never too busy to make time for you. Do you want to come to supper? We haven't seen you for ages.'

'That would be lovely. Will Mouse be there?'

I smiled. Talk about the odd couple, but they had a strong bond.

'And Hades. Come straight over and we'll have the wine open.'

I bought a pre-roasted chicken for supper and made some mashed potatoes to go with a medley of vegetables. I carved the chicken and put it in a low oven to keep warm. Mouse made some gravy and stole pieces of roast chicken skin which he shared with Hades. We sat in the kitchen drinking a glass of wine until Flo knocked on the door. She came in looking windswept and dramatic with her actor's cloak flung around her shoulders. Her formidable bulk added to her overall attraction. She looked like a famous opera singer and she worked with dead people. Quite a resumé.

Flo put a bottle on the table and sank into an armchair with a sigh of relief, kicking off her shoes and resting her swollen ankles on a pouffe upholstered in a piece of

Persian carpet. She reached forward and tried to massage her toes, but failed and lay back in her chair, panting. Hades jumped up on the pouffe and lay on top of her feet. She groaned in pain. Mouse lifted him off again and took him to the sofa.

'Long day?' I said.

'Eternal. That D.I. Antrim is a slave driver and ruder than anything. The things he said to me today, about my weight affecting my work, well, it's just uncalled for.'

She took the scrunchy off her bun and tried to tidy her hair into a new one. A fat tear escaped from her eye and sat like a jewel on her embroidered bodice. Mouse jumped up from the sofa and sat on the pouffe next to her feet. He took one in both hands and massaged it gently.

'You are beautiful and clever,' he said. 'If you were my age, I'd be in love with you.'

A lump in my throat prevented me from agreeing. Mouse sometimes behaved like a teenager, and sometimes like a wise man, but he had an enormous heart. He made me feel proud to be his surrogate mother. Flo beamed and swallowed.

'Thank you. I'd be lucky to be in love with you at any age. I'm just being silly. I know I'm overweight, but it hurt my feelings.'

'He had no right to insult you,' I said. 'You're the best pathologist in Seacastle.'

She managed a snort of laughter.

'Thanks. I'm also the only pathologist in Seacastle, but you knew that.'

'Seriously though, I may have a solution to the Antrim problem. George asked me to help him solve the case today. If he manages to impress the Superintendent, Antrim will go back to Brighton,' I said.

'Wow! That's amazing. He must be desperate. I hope you said yes,' said Mouse.

'Of course. We're practically experts now. But we'll need some inside information if we're going to work this out. First, we need to prove ourselves innocent.'

Flo rolled her eyes.

'An ambush. I should have known.'

'I told you the truth,' said Mouse. 'You are beautiful and clever. It wasn't a plan.'

'Thank you, sweetheart. I'm talking about your sleuthing colleague, Ms Bowe.'

'Will you help us? I know you're not keen on George,' I said.

'That's true, but D.I. Antrim is much worse. I'd love to see him knocked off his pedestal.'

She scratched her head and shut her eyes as if to remember something.

'Okay, this is strictly confidential and off the record, so no blabbing. I carried out Lance Emerald's autopsy today. There's no doubt he was strangled with Mouse's Brighton and Hove Albion scarf, but he didn't appear to have struggled.'

'You're right. The dressing room is tiny and you would have expected him to knock over things when he fought for his life. It looked exactly as it did when I left Lance there after my interview.'

Even as I said this, something nagged at me which I couldn't bring to the front of my brain.

'Also, I didn't find any skin cells under his fingernails which is odd. I've sent his blood off to the laboratory for them to do a tox screen, along with a sample from the whisky bottle we found in his room.'

'You think he may have been drugged first?'

'Possibly. I'll know when I get the results.'

And then I remembered.

'What did you do with his ring?' I said.

'What ring? He didn't have one on either hand,' said Flo.

'Frank Sinatra gave Lance a ring years ago and he's recently started to wear it. He told me he had terminal cancer and he wanted to show it off before he died.'

'He definitely had cancer. His lungs were black. But he wasn't wearing a ring.'

'So, whoever killed him stole the ring? Who knew about it?' said Mouse.

'Anyone who read the local paper,' I said. 'My article included a paragraph about the gift and Jasmine's photograph showcased the ring.'

'That doesn't narrow down the suspect list much,' said Flo.

'And how did my scarf get there?' said Mouse.

'I suspect you left it in the Shanty that night we heard Lance singing. Maybe he picked it up, or someone else?' I said.

'If he had it in the dressing room, maybe the killing was opportunistic and not planned,' said Flo. 'But if someone drugged him, it doesn't make sense.'

'When I served him a whisky, I almost finished the bottle. Do you know if the bottle was replaced with another?'

'No, but I can find out.'

'Who are the main suspects right now?' said Mouse.

Flo laughed.

'Antrim told me he suspected the two of you.'

'In cahoots, or one of us acting alone?' I said.

'It was her,' said Mouse, pointing at me. 'I'm only a boy.'

'What sort of idiot uses a scarf with his name on it?' I said, and we both chortled.

'It's not funny,' said Flo. 'There's plenty of circumstantial evidence against both of you.'

'And what possible motive could I have? He told me he was dying. Why kill him when he didn't have long to live?'

'Someone who needed him to die within a certain timeframe? Or someone who didn't know he was dying?' I said. 'He told me about his cancer off the record because he didn't want anyone to pity him. He wanted to go out with a bang.'

'Professional jealousy?' said Mouse. 'Hunter Norman hated Lance. He had waited years for the spotlight, but he couldn't beat Lance, the punters' favourite.'

'Maybe he got sick of waiting?' I said.

'Strangulation is an intensely personal way to kill someone, and you have to be very determined. Somebody hated him,' said Flo.

'But who? The other contestants don't even know him. Why would they hate him?' I said.

'That's just it. So far there are no other suspects,' said Flo.

'Most of them have stage names. We need to find out who they really are in order to make a list.'

'We'd better do some digging before we get arrested,' I said.

Chapter 12

I stared upwards at the tower block, one of the many that lay along the shore on the east end of Seacastle, each one more opulent than the last. The original blocks of council flats had long since been converted into holiday apartments or seaside homes from home. This older block had a bohemian air, lent to it by the plants which tumbled over the edge of balconies, and the deckchairs and bicycles propped against the balcony walls. The herring gulls down on the beach had surrounded a small fishing boat and were demanding the scraps from a fisherman who, unhurried by this squawking chorus, gutted some herring he had netted out to sea.

As I waited outside the front door for Harry to turn up, I wondered if I would ever afford to move into one of these high-rise flats instead of the Grotty Hovel. Against my will, I had become fond of my little house with its evil back garden. Then, with a start, I realised I probably couldn't take Hades with me. Most of these buildings' rules did not allow pets, and I couldn't bear the thought of parting with him. Not that I'd seen him for days. The ratbag had sneaked next door to hang out in his old digs with Helen and Olivia. Mouse often joined him, so I had begun to feel a tiny bit sorry for myself.

Harry arrived late. Rare for him, but I didn't comment. I noticed the bags under his eyes and the downturn of his lips and my heart went out to him. I buried my troubles deep within, and gave him my absolute best full-beam smile. His expression softened. I gave him a hug and held on tight while he sniffed my hair and nuzzled my neck.

'Hello, partner,' he said. 'Ready for another episode of *What's My Antique*?'

'Sure am. What floor are we on?'

'Eighth, I think. Ring a doorbell.'

After ringing three, a man's voice answered and he pressed the buzzer for us to enter the lobby.

'Where's the lift?' I said.

'Over there. Oh…'

We both stood in front of the lift staring at the out of order notice stuck on the doors.

'Eight floors?' I said. 'Good thing I've given up smoking.'

'And how do we take things down eight floors?'

'Maybe there'll be a cabinet full of Faberge Eggs?'

Harry grunted and started up the stairs. Eight floors up we sat on the top step panting and getting our breath back. I stroked Harry's face and he leaned it against the palm of my hand.

'You look exhausted. Have you managed to get hold of Nick?'

'No. He's disappeared again. It's so frustrating. I just want to know he's okay.'

'Maybe George could help?'

'George? Isn't he busy keeping the streets of Seacastle free from crime?'

'Actually, he's been replaced for this murder case due to a conflict of interest.'

'Oh, and why's that?'

I grinned.

'Because Mouse and I are suspects.'

'I think you'd better tell me about it another time. I'm not in the mood for twenty-questions.'

'Okay. But he's bouncing off the walls in the station. Flo says he's unbearable. He needs something to do.'

'I don't think it's advisable with our situation the way it is.'

'I guess you're right, but let me know if you change your mind.'

Harry stood up and pulled me to my feet.

'Let's see if there's anything worth carrying.'

The door opened only after Harry gave it a bump with his shoulder. The frame had a brown substance on it which had made the door stick. As I entered the apartment, I had the urge to vomit, due to the overwhelming smell of cigarettes. It was as if we had walked into an ashtray left after a hard night at the pub.

'This is gruesome,' said Harry, poking a stained sofa. 'None of this stuff is resalable. They just want us to clear the flat for free, and worse, without a lift.'

I swallowed and tried to get my bearings. The carpet had dozens of pockmarks from cigarette burns and the ceilings were all stained yellow by nicotine. And then I saw it, an Odeon clamshell lamp in milk glass, covered in a layer of tar, but still beautiful.

'Can you take that lamp shade down for me?'

'The one with the chain? Sure. I'll get a chair from the kitchen.'

I wandered around the flat, avoiding touching any of the revolting furniture, and I found several more beautiful light fittings including a schoolhouse pendant light with brass down-rod, a Murano milk glass flower light, and a white swirl Murano glass mushroom lamp. I showed them to Harry and got him to take them all down. In a small sideboard in the sitting room, I also found a vintage Fostoria Winburn aqua blue milk glass creamer, a Westmoreland milk glass sawtooth pattern butter dish, a Fenton Art glass periwinkle hobnail jar, and a ruffled ginger jar vase. Whoever owned the flat had been a serious milk glass collector and milk glass had exploded in value the last few years.

'Is this stuff any good?' said Harry.

'It will be, once we've removed the coat of nicotine. I'll get the troops in to give it a wash, and it will be as good as new. We'll make bank on this clearance, I promise.'

'And how do we get it downstairs?'

'Very carefully.'

It took us three trips up and down the stairs to take the items to the ground floor. Luckily, we found a couple of large buckets and using the filthy covers from the chairs we wrapped the glass to protect it from breaking or chipping on the way down stairs. Finally, we got all of our booty loaded into crates and wrapped in blankets at the back of the van. I smelled my hands and wrinkled my nose in disgust.

'I smell like an ashtray.'

'Me too. I'm glad you don't smoke anymore.'

'So am I. The van stinks too.'

We drove to Second Home with the windows down, but I still felt nauseous. Harry stared straight ahead, but he patted my leg after a while.

'How's that sister of yours?'

'Oh, same as ever. Condescending, critical, opinionated.'

'Are you making an effort?'

'I've lent her Hades.'

'You mean he's deserted. What a toerag that cat is! Does Helen have expensive cat food or something?'

'I think he does it on purpose to make me cross. Or she does. I'm trying to rise above. And Mouse likes Olivia so he's spending a lot of time over there too.'

'Is he now? Does that mean you could do with some company?'

I grinned.

'Perhaps. Are you offering?'

'Are you asking?'

I jumped out of the van without replying and started to unload the boxes, helped by Mouse who had seen us pull up to the kerb. Harry winked at me as I worked and started to whistle. It gladdened my heart to hear it. Before he drove off, he gave me a squeeze.

'I'll be back soon. I promise. Just got to keep looking while the trail is warm.'

'Be careful.'

'It's not dangerous.'

'It is to your feelings. Don't get your hopes up too high.'

'I won't.'

'I'll come with you if you need me.'

'Not this time. See you soon.'

After he'd gone, Mouse came up to me.

'Are you two okay?' he said.

'We will be. Life gets in the way of happy endings sometimes.'

'Is there anything I can do?'

'You could make me a cup of tea. I need to wash my hands and get this taste out of my mouth.'

Chapter 13

The next morning, I enlisted Ghita and Roz's help to clean the lamps which had a thick coating of nicotine tar and fly excrement. Roz had been out fishing on her husband Ed's boat and same straight to Second Home. She cycled up the street, her mop of blonde curls streaming behind her, her mermaid dress of many layers in peril of getting caught in the chain. She breezed into the shop bringing a smell of the sea with her. After giving me a big hug, she admired the photographs of local celebrities I had put on the wall.

'These look fantastic. It seems like centuries ago, doesn't it? We'll soon be vintage ourselves at this rate. Where's Ghita? Still snuggled up to Rohan and Kieron? Who could've predicted that strange threesome?'

'Steady on. They're not exactly a ménage à trois.'

'Stranger things have happened. This is Seacastle you know. What about that odd murder at the theatre? They say another tribute act killed him, out of jealousy.'

I tried to keep a straight face.

'Mouse and I are suspects.'

Roz guffawed.

'Of course you are. How do you manage it? I told you I was getting Jessica Fletcher vibes.'

'Who's Jessica Fletcher?' said Ghita, pushing her way through the door with a large cake tin. 'Give me a hand. This thing is heavy.'

Roz took the tin from her with zero effort and took it upstairs.

'Be careful. It's my new invention for cake of the week. Tipsy Cherry cake.'

'That sounds dangerous as well as delicious,' I said. 'Put a label on it with a warning that it contains alcohol. We don't want any alcoholics breaking their bans.'

'But the alcohol evaporates during cooking.'

'All the same. Better safe than sorry. What did you use? Cherry brandy?'

'Heering cherry liqueur.'

'Can we try some?' said Roz.

'Shouldn't we clean the lamps first?' said Ghita.

'I can't believe you don't know who Jessica Fletcher is,' I said.

'Yuck. These stink,' said Roz. 'Did the person who owned the flat die of lung cancer?'

'They're more likely to be embalmed in nicotine like the lamps,' said Ghita.

'I don't know if they're dead or not,' I said. 'But these objects were free, and with a swift wash, they could be beautiful and easy to sell.'

Soon we had the glass lamps soaking in a mix of vinegar and hot water, and were rubbing them down with sponge pan scrubbers to remove the cigarette tar.

'That flat must have been disgusting. The smell is making me feel sick,' said Ghita.

She moved to the door to take a breath of fresh air and picked up the post which had been dropped though the letter box.

'You can't begin to imagine,' I said. 'Can you check the post for anything important and put the junk in the bin please?'

She scrutinised the envelopes and shook her head.

'Only junk mail here,' she said, and went behind the counter to put them in the bin. 'Oh, look at these! Are they the trimmings from the photographs you framed?'

'Yes, I didn't chop off anything important, I hope.'

A lightbulb went on in my head, and I went to get my mobile.

'What is it?' said Roz.

'Just something I need to check.'

Jasmine answered her telephone almost immediately.

'Isn't it dreadful about Lance?' she said. 'I'm sorry you had to go through the police interview.'

'Can I ask you a question?'

'Sure.'

'Where did you take the photograph of Lance?'

'The one in our article? In his dressing room. He wouldn't pose anywhere else. And he made a pass at me.'

'You should be flattered. He targeted teenagers.'

'I hope you're joking,' said Jasmine.

'Sorry, that was inappropriate. My bad. Can you bring your laptop to the Vintage and show me the originals? I'll buy you a coffee.'

'Make it a pot of tea and it's a deal. I'm just down the road at Boots. I'll get my prescription and be with you shortly.'

I went back to help the girls with the lamps. The vinegar solution worked a treat on the nicotine deposits. The lamps looked almost new. I would have to get them rewired, but I could charge a decent amount for them if Grace didn't make me an offer for the lot. She and Max had acquired many new clients due to the exodus of people from Brighton because of the expense. The cheaper cost of buying a house in Seacastle left them with lots of spending money. Grace's shop always had high-end pieces and her clients liked to pay high prices so they could show off to their friends.

We left the lamps to dry on some newspaper and migrated upstairs to try Ghita's new recipe. Before long, I heard the bell clanging downstairs and Jasmine came in. She headed upstairs with her Mac laptop under her arm. I couldn't help noticing she had expensive shoes on too. I had seen them in the window of a boutique down Grace's end of the high street, and I knew how much they cost. How could she afford them? Her income as a photographer must be a lot more than I imagined. I made her a pot of tea while she sat chatting to the girls.

'Do you want a slice of Tipsy Cherry cake?' I said. 'It's Ghita's new recipe.'

'No thanks. I just had lunch. I haven't got much time. Let me upload the original photographs I took of Lance on my screen, and you can look at them.'

I took the laptop and sat in the window seat to examine them one by one. Now the cropped parts had been restored, I could see the interior of Lance's revolting dressing room with its stained walls and tatty mirror. I increased the magnification and looked over every inch of each photograph. And then I saw it.

'Bingo!' I said.

'What have you found using my clue?' said Ghita, puffing up with self-importance. She looked like a sparrow who'd just swallowed a worm.

'I've found Mouse's scarf. Look there. In the corner of the dressing room hanging on the nail.'

'And what does Mouse's scarf have to do with anything?' said Jasmine.

'It's the murder weapon,' I said. 'But don't tell anyone you know that. It might be important to keep quiet for now.'

'But how does that help. Surely if Mouse owns it, that points at him as the killer,' said Roz.

'No. It proves that anyone could have used it. Jasmine photographed it in Lance's dressing room a couple of days before the murder.'

'I did? Well, that was clever of me,' said Jasmine, without enthusiasm.

'Can you forward it to the police station,' I said.

'I'd rather you did it,' she said. 'I don't want to get mixed up in a murder inquiry.'

'Sure. Just put it in the Dropbox and I'll send it to George.'

'Isn't Inspector Antrim in charge of the case?' said Roz.

'Not for long.'

Chapter 14

After I texted George the photograph of Mouse's scarf in Lance's dressing room, he texted me back to invite himself to dinner. I thought about refusing, but his defence of Mouse had made me hopeful of them getting on better. I replied and told him he could come if he promised to call Mouse by his preferred moniker and not Andy. I could almost feel George fuming, but he agreed. I shut up shop and paid a rapid visit to the supermarket.

I pulled up outside my house in my faithful Mini, to find Harry loitering by the front door. My heart leapt in my chest as he came over to help me carry the bags inside. He gave me a soft kiss on the lips which almost made me drop the eggs on the pavement.

'Hello, partner. Long time no see.'

'What about the clearance we just did together?'

'It feels like forever, and I thought you might be lonely.'

'Not tonight, but the more the merrier. Hungry?'

'What's for dinner?'

'I'm planning on whipping up a fish pie. You can stay if you want, but I must warn you; George is coming too.'

'And what does he want?'

'Don't be grumpy. I'm helping him with a murder inquiry.'

'Again? Can't he cope by himself?'

'It's sort of my fault. Well, mine and Mouse's.'

He laughed.

'What a family! Why don't you tell me all about it while I peel the potatoes?'

Mouse gave Harry a friendly hug and then he chopped the onions while Harry peeled the potatoes in the sink. I made a white sauce for the fish pie from the milk I had used to cook the fish. We told Harry about the murder of Lance Emerald, and the presence of Mouse's scarf in his dressing room.

'No wonder George is not allowed to investigate,' said Harry. 'Your whole family is involved in the murder. Even your niece could be involved. Wasn't she at the theatre as well?'

'Don't be ridiculous. Olivia is afraid of spiders. She's not going to strangle someone to death with a scarf.'

The doorbell rang and Mouse ran to answer it. George stood outside with Helen and Olivia; his expression inscrutable.

'I found these people outside,' he said. 'Do they belong to you?'

'You know they do. Don't you recognise Olivia. I suppose she is a lot taller than the last time you met.'

'He's joking,' said Helen. 'He invited us to supper with you.'

'Did he now? Luckily, I can add some prawns to the fish pie to pad it out a bit. Come in and meet Harry.'

'Harry?' said George. 'I haven't seen you for ages.'

To my surprise, he shook Harry's hand with a warm smile. Helen's mouth fell open and stayed there, until Harry shook her hand too.

'I'm Harry, Tanya's business partner and, um, yes.'

'You're Harry? I'm Olivia, Tanya's niece. I've heard about you from Mouse.'

'All good I hope.'

'Naturally,' said Mouse.

I felt a little overwhelmed with the potential flashpoints lurking in the evening ahead, and sank into a chair. Mouse yelped and ran into the kitchen to shoo Hades away from the fish pie. He slipped out through the cat flap with a cube of haddock he had stolen from the pie dish. George didn't notice as he had assumed the role of host. He poured Helen and Harry glasses of wine and started to quiz Olivia on the talent competition.

I returned to my white sauce which had luckily not spoiled and sprinkled in a fish stock cube. Mouse tested the potatoes and finding them cooked, carried them to the table to mash them with milk, pepper and butter. I smiled at his domesticity. He had been a reluctant cook at first, but now I couldn't keep him out of the kitchen. I wondered if Rohan and Kieron could take him on for a few shifts a week. What girl could resist a boy who could cook modern fusion dishes?

Once the pie sat on the top shelf of the oven, I put some frozen peas and green beans on to cook, and went to pour myself a glass of wine. Helen sat on the armchair with a bemused expression on her face as Harry and George talked in low voices together. Mouse and Olivia were bent over the laptop giggling at something on

YouTube. He glowed with happiness. I noticed that George referred to him as Mouse when he was talking to Harry. Mouse had noticed too. His eyes shone as he looked at his father. I felt as if someone had emptied a vial of happiness down the chimney of the Grotty Hovel and infected us all.

We finished every scrap of fish pie and my emergency supply of chocolate ice cream before Helen dragged Olivia next door to bed. Harry and Mouse watched an action movie and George helped me to wash up while we discussed the case.

'Thanks for the photo of the dressing room,' he said. 'That will stop Antrim targeting Mouse. He's still pretending to believe you have something to do with it, but he's the only one at the station. Have you got any leads yet?'

'Shouldn't I be asking you that question?'

'Come on. You know I'm not supposed to be digging into the case.'

'I need to finish my interviews of the contestants for Jasmine. That will give me the perfect excuse to question them about their relationships with Lance. I have heard Hunter Norman and Lance were at loggerheads over Lance's star billing. Maybe I can find out how deep his animosity ran.'

'The easy access to Lance's dressing room from outside the theatre is a problem. What if someone came in, killed him and left again?'

'Wouldn't someone have seen them? There were a lot of people back stage for the rehearsals that day.'

'And what about Lance's past? He has a criminal record.'

I stopped to look at George.

'A record? What for? You should have told me this before.'

'I didn't know. I can get you a copy, but it's a paper file, so it will take me a while to organise.'

'Okay.'

'Don't let anyone see it or tell anyone you have it. Tell Harry I'll get back to him on his problem. I presume he's staying here tonight?'

'It's none of your business. I don't mind sharing my information on the case with you, but my personal life is out of bounds.'

'Harry's a nice man, but you'll change your mind. I'll wait.'

'Night George.'

He left after shaking hands with Harry and Mouse and giving me a peck on the cheek. Mouse looked around the room and headed for the stairs muttering about being green and hairy.

'I thought he would never go,' said Harry.

Then he saw my expression.

'George, not Mouse. Although I've been waiting for us to be alone all night.'

'Did you get on with Helen? I was distracted by the cooking and couldn't help you.'

'Not bad. She didn't say much. Just sat looking at me with her jaw resting on her chest. I don't think she expected to see George and me having dinner together.'

I smiled.

'I don't expect she did. She's probably lying in bed working out what to say to me tomorrow, but too shocked by our ménage à trois to get her thoughts straight.'

'Is George the elephant in the room?' said Harry.

'No, I sent him home, because I wanted to be alone with you. That part of my life is over.'

'Why don't you come and sit on the sofa with me and tell me about the next part?'

'Or we could go to bed and chat up there? Mouse won't mind and Hades is out hunting.'

'I thought you'd never ask.'

Chapter 15

After Harry had left in his van, I made myself a cup of tea and stood at the back door listening to the sparrows quarrelling in the brambles. Hades slunk between my legs deigning to rub against them momentarily. I didn't bother to try and stroke him. I had grown bored of those games and I didn't want to spill my tea. His fur gleamed in the weak sunlight and he appeared to have gained weight. No doubt my sister fed him as often as he asked, foolish woman.

Mouse came up behind me and gave me a hug.

'How was your sleepover?' he said. 'I heard you talking for hours.'

'We had a lot to say. I hope we didn't keep you awake.'

'No. I had some research to do.'

'About what?'

'Stuff. Shall I make you some toast?'

I knew better then to inquire further, and the thought of hot buttered toast made me salivate.

'Yum. Yes please.'

A slight nip in the air advertised the coming of autumn as I walked to the theatre. Mouse came with me as far as King Street, and then he crossed the road and headed for the shop. I walked around the theatre to the stage door and met Cynthia opening it up. She wore black and her face bore evidence of mourning, being puffy with swollen eyes. I had not realised she cared for Lance. Before he died, she had struggled to conceal her dislike of his constant demands and abhorrent behaviour. I needed to know more about their relationship and I decided to take advantage of her fragile state to see if she might tell me, now he had died.

'Hello, ducks,' she said. 'Are you here to do some more interviews?'

'That's right. But first I'd like to ask you some questions if I may? For my general background article on the competition. Would that be okay?'

She tucked some stray grey hairs behind her ear, her thinning hair and pink scalp more obvious in daylight. I felt a spasm of pity for her. She had obviously been exquisitely pretty in her youth, but age had robbed her of her confidence, if not her looks. Her bright blue eyes were bloodshot in her heart-shaped face, and her neck hung in folds which disappeared into her silk neck scarf. She wore an ice blue jumper with obvious pilling and a drab tweed skirt over thick nylon tights. Her tiny feet were swollen and lumpy in her shapeless shoes.

'That's a beautiful brooch,' I said, when she caught me staring at her.

She beamed.

'Isn't it? If you want a cup of coffee, I'll tell you where I got it.'

She shuffled ahead of me up the stairs and along the corridor into her stuffy office. I touched the radiator and found it scalding hot despite still being August. Then I remembered Lance's body, still warm in his room. The police had assumed someone wanted to disguise the time of death, but maybe the reason was more prosaic.

'Ouch, that radiator's hot.' I said. 'Should it be on?'

'No wonder it's so tropical in here. Someone must have flipped the switch by mistake. It's easy to do. It's in a panel of other ones for lighting and curtains and so on. I don't know who designed the theatre, but the electrics are all a bit of a bodge job.'

I thought of Goose and his young family, and decided to recommend him to Reg, although it seemed unlikely that he had any money to pay for upgrading the electrics.

'I haven't been backstage yet. I'd love a tour.'

'I'm sure Reg would be happy to show you around.'

'Are you going to tell me where you got your brooch?'

'Lance. I'm wearing it in his memory today. We used to be an item in ancient times.'

Her lower lip wobbled.

'You went out with Lance? And he gave you a brooch. That doesn't sound like the man I met.'

'He used to be different. He loved his life and his work, but his ambition got the better of him. And his taste for young girls. He broke my heart, the bastard.'

'I'm so sorry. Was that around the time he sang in the Balentine Brothers' duo?'

'Yes, around then.'

'Can you remember the other brother's real name?'

Her hand flew to her neck and she started to fiddle with the knot in her scarf.

'His name? Um, I… I'm sorry. I can't. I only knew him by his stage name; Greg Balentine. Almost no one in showbusiness or theatre uses their real name you know. If your name is Joe Bloggs and there is another one registered, you have to change your name or add another letter.'

'He must have been disappointed when Lance decided to go out on his own.'

'It destroyed him. He gave up his career.'

'Is that when Lance started to change?'

'I guess so. I didn't realise how much until he dumped me out of the blue.'

'Mixed memories then. Did you hate him?'

'Not any more. I tolerated him. That's about it. Do you want that cup of tea?'

'I'm supposed to interview Hunter, so I'll take a rain check on the tea, thank you.'

'No problem. Hunter is not easy either, you know.'

'I have been warned.'

She gave me a watery smile. I wondered how she had met the Balentine Brothers. I needed to do some more research, but I didn't want to upset her by overdoing the questions. Perhaps Reg would know.

'He's moved into Lance's dressing room,' said Sammy Singh, when I asked him where Hunter Norman had gone.

'Isn't that a little odd?' I asked. 'I mean, a bit soon after…'

'Oh, he doesn't care. He just wants to be alone.'

'Marlene complex?'

'Or superiority complex.'

'Thanks Sam.'

Hunter had a glass of whisky in his hand when I arrived at the dressing room. I had the weirdest sensation of déja vu as he sneered at me from the chaise longue. At least he had clothes on.

'Well, look who it is. The suspect come to see me. How nice.'

'The police have cleared me and I'm here to interview you,' I said.

'Can I claim the fifth?'

'No, that's only in America. You have to answer all my questions.'

He tutted, but his face remained expressionless. I wondered if he had any personality behind the blank exterior.

'No, I don't, but I might give you a scoop for the local rag.'

He swirled the whisky around in his glass and took a large swig. I don't often lose my temper, but a red mist descended for a second and I went for the jugular.

'Did you murder Lance Emerald?'

Hunter's eyes almost popped out of his head, and he spat out his mouthful of whisky.

'What sort of a question is that?'

'Well, I heard you two were bitter rivals, and you couldn't beat him in a fair competition, so naturally...'

I trailed off and let my pen hover over my notepad.

'Who told you that?'

He planted the glass on the rickety side table and leaned forward pointing his finger at me.

'You're not much of a journalist, are you? Everybody knows these things are fixed. They have a lot in common with professional wrestling; the golden boy, the crowd favourites, the evil rival, and the no-hopers who make up the numbers. Lance won because he was the oldies' favourite, our best customers by far. We weren't allowed to beat him and disappoint them.'

'Which role did you play in this cast?'

'Do you have to ask? My role was pantomime villain.'

'Was? What are you now?'

He sneered.

'Cynthia owes me. Why do you think I've got the star's dressing room? Any other stupid questions, or are you finished?'

His smug expression triggered me, but I stayed calm, as I knew he was vulnerable in his self-righteous anger.

'Did you know Lance had terminal cancer?' I said.

His jaw muscles tightened and the blood drained from his features. He jumped up and screamed into my face.

'You're lying! He couldn't have.'

I didn't move, even as his spittle flew into my face. I stared him down, and he stumbled backwards putting out his hand to stop himself falling onto the couch. His mouth worked, but no sound came out.

'You didn't know?'

'Cynthia would have told me. She always...'

He stopped and dropped his head into his hands.

'Go away,' he said, his voice muffled.

'But I haven't interviewed you yet.'

'That's your problem. I'm sure the others have plenty to say. Why don't you ask them?'

'It's obviously not a good time right now. I'll be back.'

I shut the door and stood out in the passageway taking a couple of deep breaths. Cindy Gold tottered up to me on her high heels.

'Have you finished interviewing the men yet? Only we're here too, you know. And now that Lance has shuffled off the mortal coil, you need to make an effort or you might miss the next rising star.'

She pushed me aside and let herself into Hunter's room. She had a point. I needed to talk to the girls. Knowing Lance, he would have made enemies amongst them too. And I hadn't talked to Reg yet.

Chapter 16

Flo had promised to let me know when she got the results back from the fingerprinting of Lance's dressing room and the tox screen from his blood. I still imagined D.I. Antrim would find a way to make me look guilty just to get at George. I found it hard to relax, and paced the shop every day, unable to take joy in my stock. Roz came in more often, as she tended to when she knew I couldn't settle. She made us coffee and told me the most extraordinary gossip from all around Seacastle. I never knew so much happened behind closed doors.

'Have you spoken to Marge about Lance,' she said, out of the blue.

'Marge? Hairdresser Marge? What's she got to do with Lance?'

'A little birdie told me she used to tread the boards in her youth. Our Marge was quite a gal from what I hear.'

I laughed.

'Where on earth did you pick up that gem? You're astonishing. I'm surprised Ryan Wells hasn't tried to recruit you for MI5 yet.'

She gave me a slightly crazy look and tapped the side of her nose.

'And how do you know he hasn't?'

I shook my head. Ryan and Joy ran our favourite local pub up on the cliffs overlooking Pirate's Harbour. They were forever travelling to Prague and other random places for 'work'. Ryan had had an unexplained accident which left him in a wheelchair before he came to live in Seacastle, but he still disappeared for days on these errands. The less they told us, the more we speculated, but what would you expect of a small town like Seacastle, with master gossipers like Roz Murray?

'Because you can't keep a secret to save your life?'

'Hm. Well, there's that I suppose. But seriously, you should go and see Marge. You need a haircut anyway and she did a great job last time.'

True. She sculpted my hair into a film star bouffant which left Harry tongue-tied. I looked up their number on my phone and rang to make an appointment. The snotty girl on reception told me they had a cancellation for four o'clock with Marge, if I could get there in time. I could almost see her unsmiling, bitchy face as she admitted it. I thanked her profusely and assured her that, no, I wouldn't dare to be late. Heaven forbid!

Roz raised an eyebrow at my sarcastic tone and I waggled mine back at her. I didn't feel like being polite to someone who was just plain nasty. I decided to prompt Marge's memory rather than ask her any specific questions. As with most hairdressers, she had a habit of asking questions rather than answering them, but finding out where people are going on their holidays must lose its shine after thirty years. I gambled on her interest being piqued by the Lance Emerald murder, and the flood gates to open without me needing to ask intrusive questions. I would pretend to be Roz-like in my search for gossip so she wouldn't be suspicious.

After lunch, we had a visit from Grace inquiring about our gorgeous milk glass lamps and tableware. She made a list of everything we had rescued and stored it in her phone. Instead of rushing off, she came upstairs and had a coffee with us. She seemed preoccupied and not the usual abrasive character who rushed into the shop, slammed down a wad of cash and strode out again. She ordered a pot of jasmine tea and picked at a slice of elderflower and pomegranate cake, Ghita's latest cake of the week. I sent Roz and Mouse downstairs to mind the shop. I could feel the resentment emanating from Roz's back as she descended the stairs. She couldn't stand missing out on gossip. I would usually have tolerated Roz's voracious appetite for novelty, but something about Grace's manner made me shoo her away.

'Are you okay,' I said. 'You seem a little preoccupied.'

'A young man came into the shop and forced me to give him the cash I had in my handbag. That's why I can't pay you right now. I thought I was okay, but I feel a little shaky.'

'Have you called the police?'

'Of course not.'

I scratched my head at this answer. She sipped her tea unconcerned.

'What do mean? That's the first thing you do when you get robbed. He might have left finger prints in the shop. They can find and arrest him.'

'We never used the police in Hong Kong. They were not trustworthy.'

She crossed her arms and I didn't push it, even though I had the opposite impression of policing in Hong Kong. I had seen a documentary which claimed they were exemplary.

'Would you recognise him if you saw him again?'

'Most definitely. He had a shaved head and tattoos and a big ring on his finger.'

'What sort of ring?'

'Garnet. Set in Gold.'

The hairs on my arms stood on end. I rubbed them, hoping she hadn't noticed.

'Are you sure?' I said.

'Of course. I know what I saw.'

'I'm sorry that happened to you. I'm off to the hairdressers soon, I can walk you back to your shop if you'd like.'

She smiled.

'I'd like that. I'm sure he's off drinking my money in some bar, but I'm not ready to walk back by myself. First let me finish my tea and cake. I would like a slice to take back for Max as well. This is really delicious.'

I left her upstairs and cornered Mouse at the downstairs toilet.

'Do you know Cracker, Goose's friend?'

He smirked.

'Why? Do you need him to burgle a house for you?'

'I think he just mugged Grace.'

'Oh.'

'I need his real name.'

'Goose?'

'No. Cracker.'

'Are you going to turn him in?'

'I think he may be connected to Lance's murder.'

'Lance? I don't understand. Why would he murder Lance?'

'I have no idea. But I need his real name so I can give it to George.'

'What about D.I. Antrim? Isn't he in charge of the murder?'

'Ah, but this is a mugging, and George is still dealing with muggings and petty theft.'

'I'll text Goose. I'm not sure he knows it though.'

'And what's Goose's real name?'

'I can't remember. Gary something?'

'You lot are hopeless.'

Mouse shrugged.

'I'll forward it to you when I get it.'

I walked Grace along the high street to her shop with my arm linked in hers. She was tiny, even shorter than Ghita, and was fine boned like a little songbird. I felt like an elephant walking with a gazelle. Her black hair shone in the sun and it struck me how pretty she was. I'd never really noticed before. We were always so busy negotiating that we'd never had time to talk before. I made a mental note to invite her to join us more often. She had come to Ghita's Fat Fighter's classes, but she found us all a little frivolous for her taste.

I left her at the door of her shop and continued along to the hairdresser's. The receptionist greeted me with a brittle smile.

'Mrs Bowe. Marge will be with you shortly.'

'Ms Bowe.'

'Whatever.'

She muttered it under her breath, but I heard her. I didn't let it distract me. I pretended to read a magazine article extolling the wonders of Meghan Markle and waited for my turn.

Chapter 17

Marge came bustling up to me with a broad smile on her face.

'Tanya? I remember you. We spoke about the Conrads after Mel got murdered. I couldn't believe who did it. It just goes to show.'

She didn't tell me what it went to show, but I knew what she meant.

'That's right. And you're wearing another one of your fabulous cardigans. I don't know how you do it.'

Her cheeks went pink with pleasure, and she guided me through to the mirrors. She put a cape around my neck and fluffed out my hair.

'What are we doing today?' she said.

'Oh, just a trim and set,' I said. 'I want to look glamorous.'

After the trainee washed my hair, I sat looking at myself in the mirror, wondering why the lighting in hairdresser's always seemed to show every blemish and wrinkle on my face. Marge took out a pair of razor-sharp scissors and snipped my hair with consummate skill. Then she took out the setting lotion and sprayed my hair.

Once it was in curlers, she wheeled up a helmet and timed it for twenty minutes.

'Do you want a cup of tea while we're waiting?'

I didn't. My stomach felt like a balloon full of water with all the coffee I had drunk in the Vintage. But I nodded anyway. She came back five minutes later with two cups of stewed tea with milk and sugar. I sipped mine, trying not to taste it.

'Hey,' I said. 'A friend of mine told me you used to tread the boards in your youth. Is that true?'

She giggled into her cup.

'I did. But that was a lifetime ago.'

'Do you have any old photographs from that era? I salvaged some from the Italian Café. I've got them on my phone if you want to see them.'

'Oh, yes please. Hand them it over.'

I gave her my phone and let her review the sequence several times. She lingered over them and then she held up her hand for me to wait. She disappeared into a backroom and came back with an old photograph which she gave to me. Two women in tramp's costumes were pictured on stage at a theatre. Their faces had been made up to look dirty, and their size meant I couldn't really see them, even if I squinted. She sniggered and took it back.

'Didn't you recognise me?' she said.

'That is you? Oh goodness, how funny. Who is the other lady in the photograph? Is she still around?'

I nearly said alive. Not very polite. Marge wasn't that old.

'That's Thia Dottin,' she said.

'Did you know anyone else in the business?'

'Well, there's that scoundrel Lance Emerald, of course.'

'In the Balentine Brothers? Who was the other brother?

'That's Greg, or should I say Reg, better known as Reggie Dolan, empresario extraordinaire.'

'What? Why didn't I recognise him before?'

'No wonder. He's as bald as a coot now, and as skinny as a heron.'

'I had no idea Reggie worked with Lance.'

'We all worked together actually. We travelled between the venues singing and dancing our way through the summers. It was a lot of fun while it lasted. Lance cut a swathe through the young ladies who came to see us at the shows. He couldn't control himself, not even for me.'

She gave me back the photographs and gazed into the distance. I waited for her to come back to the present. When she did, her mood had changed.

'It couldn't last,' she said, plucking at her cardigan. 'Lance had to go and spoil it. He never changed. He dedicated his whole life to making people miserable. But it came back to bite him in the end. The way I heard it, he wrecked his chance at stardom, and had to go and live in France.'

'What did he do?'

'I'm not interested in opening up old wounds. The man is dead. That's good enough for me.'

She sniffed and stood up to tip the hair dryer back off my head. She patted the curls which emitted that chemical smell so redolent of the hairdresser's art.

'Let's get those curlers out before they fry your hair.'

I moved back in front of the mirror, carrying my now lukewarm tea with me. I still sipped it valiantly, even though I couldn't stand sugar in my tea. Marge started to perform her magic with my hair and I could only stare in amazement.

'I'd love to have seen you on stage,' I said. 'If you were anything like as good at entertaining, as you are at styling, you must have been special to watch.'

'I was, dear. I had a great career ahead of me, but I had to stop just when fame beckoned me.'

She wiped her eyes with the end of a towel.

'Can we talk about something else? It's too painful for me to remember some of this stuff. Anyway, with Lance gone, it's all irrelevant now,' she said.

'Of course. Shall I tell you where I'm going to on my holidays?'

She laughed.

'I'm more interested in the comings and goings at the local nick. What's that D.I. Antrim doing down here? Is it anything to do with Lance?'

I smiled.

'Have I got some gossip for you. That's if you don't mind talking about the demise of Lance Emerald.'

'Oh, I don't mind, dearie. Good riddance to bad rubbish as far as I'm concerned. I should have done it myself if I had the courage. I'm hoping they get away with it.'

'Hold on to your hat then. I'm the prime suspect for his murder, according to D.I. Antrim, well, me and my stepson Mouse.'

Marge snorted.

'I've never done a murderer's hair before,' she said. 'Am I safe?'

'It depends on whether I like my hair style or not.'

I drew my finger across my throat and winked at her. She smiled momentarily, before frowning at my reflection.

'Seriously though. Why does he think you did it?'

'I happened to be in the theatre at the time and Lance had tried to make a pass at my stepson.'

'I hope he punched Lance. The cheek of that man. He would make a pass at a corpse.'

'Aside from me, there's a wide cast of suspects. Nearly every person in the theatre that day had a motive.'

Marge stroked her chin.

'Who's the stage manager calling the show at the Pavilion?'

'I'm not sure what you mean by calling the show?'

'They're the person providing support to the cast and technicians. Often emotional support too. Especially in a talent show. The contestants can get stressed out. They are also in charge of the cues for lights, stage entrances and so on. They know everything about everybody.'

'Oh, that'll be Cynthia. She's the mother hen.'

Marge froze, her brush in the air.

'Cynthia? What's her surname?'

'Walters, I think.'

'What does she look like?'

'Small and pretty with cornflower blue eyes. A bit like you, to be honest.'

'Anything like the other woman in my photograph?'

I took it from her again so I could examine the face of Thia Dottin. I felt some of the pieces in the puzzle arrange themselves as Marge took the phone and nodded at me.

'That's her. I'm sure of it,' I said.

'Thia is short for Cynthia, you know.'

I didn't, but it made sense. I wondered what Cynthia could tell me about Marge and Lance that Marge wouldn't tell me herself. I had a notion their past liaison could be linked to Lance's death, but I didn't know how.

'How long is it since you've met up with her?'

'Years and years, dear. Too many to remember. Not since I had to leave the act.'

'She's at the theatre every day if you want to see her.'

'I'm not sure I could bear it. Too much water under the bridge.'

'Well, you know where she is if you change your mind. Could I take a snap of your photograph? I'd like to print it out and put it in a frame in the coffee shop if you don't mind.'

'Mind? Why would I mind? Fame at last.'

Chapter 18

When I left the hairdresser's, I checked my mobile for messages and found one from Mouse. He had gone to the pub straight from work and left me a cheeky note about not waiting up. He also sent me Cracker's real name. Wayne Dawson. Cracker suited him better. He had a short fuse and a brooding sense of grievance hanging over him, like he might snap at any time. Crack!

As I drove home from the supermarket, my mobile pinged and I glanced at the screen. George had messaged me. I waited until I got home to read the full text. He had invited himself around to my house again. I nearly told him to get lost, but I also needed to discuss the day's revelations and George might have news on the forensics. Since I was theoretically still in the frame for Lance's murder, I needed to help George tie the clues together to find the real murderer. I texted him back asking when he would arrive and he replied with *about ten minute*s.

I made him take a detour via the Indian so he could bring us a curry. I did not feel like cooking, only sleuthing. As a gesture of goodwill, I laid the table and opened a nice bottle of red wine to breathe. I took the piccalilli and chutney out of the fridge and waited impatiently for George to arrive. My stomach rumbled loudly, reminding me how hungry I was. A silky body rubbed against my legs and I realised I wasn't the only one who had hunger pangs. I gave Hades a packet of his favourite food, rabbit, and he gobbled it down at high speed. Afterwards I shooed him upstairs and hid him in Mouse's room. I hadn't told George about having a cat full time yet, for some reason I couldn't put my finger on. He hated cats, but his claim to be allergic didn't ring true with me. He never started sneezing in my house despite Hades living there.

The doorbell rang and I opened the door to find George holding out his offering of fabulous smelling food. I always felt like a kingfisher when he did that. Luckily, he didn't pounce on me after I accepted the package, but he gazed at me in admiration.

'You've done something to your hair,' he said. 'You look smashing, Tan.'

I couldn't help smiling. A compliment from George was as rare as a hot day in December. We served ourselves immediately, the aroma driving me wild with hunger. I poured us a glass of wine and tried not to wolf my food down too quickly. George watched me with a smirk on his face.

'What?' I said, mildly irritated.

'I love how hungry you are. Sharon is always picking at her food. She keeps saying she's getting fat, or I'm getting fat. We're on constant weight alert.'

'I haven't eaten for hours.'

'Don't get defensive. It's a relief to hang out with a woman who eats normally.'

'That's okay. I know I'm eating fast. I'm starving today.'

'Hormones, probably,' said George.

My fork hovered in mid-air as I took in what he had said.

'And since when did you know anything about hormones. Oh, wait, Sharon, right?'

'Yup. She rams her hormones down my throat all the time. Honestly, I had no idea women were ticking timebombs.'

'Never mind. It'll get worse with the menopause.'

'She's nowhere near yet.'

'No, but I am.'

He roared with laughter.

'I may have to leave the country,' he said.

'Where is she tonight?' I asked.

'With her sister again. They're working on some business thing they're doing together with Sharon's brother-in-law. To tell the truth, it seems to be taking off.'

'But that's great. You'll soon have a second income again.'

He shook his head.

'I'm unlikely to see any of it. She has a separate bank account and doesn't contribute to the household bills.'

It was my turn to guffaw.

'That's what you get for shacking up with an entrepreneur.'

'I'm learning fast. So, Sherlock, what's the skinny on the case of Lance Emerald then?'

'You first. What's the latest forensic info? Am I off the hook yet?'

'It's looking increasingly unlikely you murdered Lance. The tox screen showed Rohypnol in Lance's blood.'

'The date rape drug?'

'Yes, it's a sedative. Colourless and odourless. Someone had added it to the whisky. It doesn't have a taste either.'

'But I served him a whisky. Weren't my fingerprints on the bottle?'

'No, but you could have wiped them off.'

I sighed.

'This isn't funny,' I said.

'You'll be glad to know Flo found several sets of fingerprints on the bottle, and none of them were yours. We traced one set on the database. They belonged to a known criminal, a young man with a history of muggings and burglaries.'

I sighed.

'Let me guess. Wayne Dawson.'

George choked on his mouthful of curry.

'How on earth did you know that?'

'Lucky guess.'

'Honestly. There's no way you guessed. Is he a friend of Andy's perchance?'

'Mouse. And yes, Mouse does know him through another friend, Goose.'

'Goose who?' said George.

'I don't know his real name. But I could find out.'

'Don't bother. We'll do it.'

'Goose is an electrician. There's no chance he's involved in Lance's murder.'

'How come you knew about Wayne?'

I filled our glasses to make him wait for the answer. I loved to push George's buttons. He watched the last drops drain into his glass, drumming his fingers on the table. I handed him his glass and he took a swig, staring at my lips as if trying to force me to speak. I took pity on him.

'I'm pretty sure he mugged Grace Wong in the street today, wearing Lance Emerald's garnet ring.'

'Why didn't you call me immediately?'

I bit my lip to prevent myself laughing.

'I had an appointment at the hairdresser's with another person linked to the inquiry.'

My smugness evident, George rolled his eyes.

'How do you do it? We should all retire and leave you to it. D.I. Antrim will be apoplectic.'

'Don't tell him then. I'm telling you so you can solve the case, not make Terry look good.'

George tipped some more rice onto his plate.

'And what did you learn at the hairdresser's?' he said.

'Earlier on in his career, Lance had a double act called the Balentines with Reg Dolan of the Pavilion theatre. The two of them used to tour with Marge Dawson from the hairdresser's, and Cynthia Walters, the stage manager for the tribute competition. There was a massive bust up years ago and the end result was a break up of the acts. Lance later took up a forced exile in Monaco. He told me about it, but not why he left Britain.'

'Do you know Reg and Cynthia?'

'I've met them a few times.'

'Any chance you can get some information on the bust-up? I'll see if I can trace Wayne Dawson. He seems like the prime suspect, but I don't want to narrow down the field too soon.'

'Ask him where he got the ring. Lance told me he got it from Frank Sinatra back in the day, so it must be quite valuable.'

'So why is he wearing it? Any thief worth his salt would have pawned it immediately, not worn it in full view of everyone.'

'Search me. He's not the sharpest tool in the box. Maybe he didn't think anyone would recognise it.'

George sat back in his chair and patted his stomach, groaning with pleasure.

'Would you like a coffee before you go?' I said.

'Have you got decaf? Sharon won't let me drink real coffee before bedtime. It keeps me awake.'

I had a sneaking admiration for Sharon. She kept George on a short rein and spent all his money. If only I'd been a little more confident, maybe we could have pulled through.

'She's right, but I don't have any. Maybe you should go home and drink one there?'

George's face fell.

'Are you throwing me out? I thought we were getting on okay again.'

'We are. That's why I'm throwing you out. Don't push your luck, and keep me posted on the search for Wayne Dawson.'

'It shouldn't take long. He's a known felon and we have an address for him. I'll get Grace Wong to give me a statement and a description, and bring him in on the mugging charge.'

'Go easy on her. She's nervous of the police. I think she and Max had some issues in Hong Kong before they left the country.'

'Thanks for the heads up.'

I held the front door open for him, and then I remembered.

'By the way, did you make any progress on finding Harry's brother?'

'Not yet, but it's early days.'

'I really appreciate you doing this for him.'

'Can I have a kiss then?'

'Not that much. Go home, George.'

Chapter 19

I walked to work to clear my head of the lurking migraine caused by imbibing too much heavy red wine. Overhead the herring gulls drifted and swooped on the fresh breeze and yelled insults at the rooks on the beach. The sea kale had lost its flowers and its formerly tender stems had become woody and inedible. George always made me drink more than I normally would. Whether he egged me on or made me nervous, I couldn't decide. I had no intention of returning to the marital home. Divorce had been good to me. The tendrils of depression lurked in our beige villa, waiting to ensnare me in their siren grasp.

On my way to Second Home, I stopped by Rohan and Kieron's new restaurant, Surfusion, which was taking shape in the old Italian café building. I peeped inside and gasped at the transformation. The taxidermy fishes they had bought from me had been taken out of their individual cases and mounted in one large tank along the inside wall, complete with kelp and seashells on a dark green background and back lit by turquoise bulbs. The montage gave me the feeling of being back in the kelp forest beneath Seacastle Bay. I wondered if the new Marine Protection Area had begun to work its magic under the sea. Maybe Roz would know, but asking her might prove a little delicate after what had happened. She had taken her time to heal after the trauma caused by the demise of the eco-warrior.

Ghita arrived on silent feet and tapped me on the shoulder, making me jump.

'Isn't it gorgeous? We're just getting all the electrics rewired and a new combi-boiler put in, and then we can start using the kitchen. I'm so excited.'

She had repressed her desire to jump around like a child on the pavement, but her mood bounced instead. I felt quite protective of her. She had taken the project to heart like everything she got involved in. Her friendship with both men had given her a new confidence, and her cooking skills had blossomed under Kieron's tutelage. I couldn't help worrying about the project though. Surfusion, subtitled seafood heaven, would be the kind of upmarket foodie place you might find in Devon, run by a sweary chef, not on the cheap end of Seacastle High Street, between two charity shops and almost opposite the Co-Op.

While I could imagine some of our friends taking the plunge and shelling out once or twice for the expensive novelty of eating there, I couldn't see where the restaurant's core clientele would come from. Who could afford to eat there once a week? I assumed Kieron knew what he was doing, but Seacastle and Brighton had almost nothing in common besides a pier and noisy herring gulls. Perhaps his loyal customers would come along the coast to Seacastle, but they would have to take the bus if they wanted more than one glass of wine.

I took Ghita's arm and walked her across the road to Second Home. She couldn't stop talking about the restaurant and the dishes and the ingredients. It took me a while to notice just how manic she sounded. Then I realised I wasn't the only one who worried about the prospects for new venture. Finally, she stopped for breath and her expression changed.

'I'm worried it won't catch on,' she said.

'It's always tricky setting up a new business,' I said. 'Look how I fretted over the Vintage and it has become a fixture in some people's schedules already.'

'But what if nobody comes? Will Rohan and Kieron have to leave again? I couldn't bear it. They've taken me in. We're like the three musketeers of cooking, fighting the odds together.'

'All for one and one for all?' I said.

'Exactly. I know it sounds silly, but I feel like I've known them for ever.'

'I know they feel the same about you. They light up when you come into the room.'

'Is it weird to be in love with them both?'

My heart broke for her as her voice caught in her throat.

'No, sweetheart. It's not weird at all. You've been looking for love for years. Nobody said it had to be conventional. Well, no one except your parents.'

'Actually, Mummy wants to meet them.'

'She does? Goodness, that's not what I expected.'

'I don't think it's what she expected either, but she and Daddy are so glad I'm happy. Maybe they'll stop trying to marry me off.'

'Now wouldn't that be wonderful?'

'And what about you? Have you decided what to do about George?'

'Oh yes. There's no going back to him now. We've grown too far apart. Sharon seems to be remoulding him into a modern man, and it's good for him.'

'What about Harry?'

'He's trying to find his brother Nick. Funnily enough George is helping him.'

'And I thought my situation was weird. Do you love him?'

'Harry? With all my heart, but we're taking it slowly. There's no rush and neither of us wants to make a mistake.'

'I really like him. He makes me feel safe.'

'He makes everyone feel safe. There's something about him. You should see him when he gets angry. People back right off when he puffs out his chest.'

'Like this?' said Ghita.

She took a deep breath and stuck out her ample bosom. I did the same and we both posed and clucked like chickens, giggling like schoolgirls.

'Exactly like that,' I said, holding my side which had developed a painful stitch. 'Except he tends to crow more.'

We both snorted and giggled. Each time we managed to stop, one of us lost control and we started again. We had to sit on the staircase to recover. Then Grace came in with a face like thunder and the mood flipped.

'How could you?' she said.

'How could I what. I don't understand.' I said.

'Are you okay?' said Ghita.

'You told the police about me,' said Grace.

Ghita's startled face looked into mine and I shook my head.

'I told George you had been mugged. He's my ex-husband. He's not just any policeman.'

'It's not fair. I told you I didn't want to report it.'

'But it's not that simple. I suppose you heard about the murder at the theatre? The ring you described was stolen from Lance Emerald's finger when he died. The young man who mugged you may be the killer.'

'A murderer? Why didn't you tell me?' said Grace

'I didn't know until last night. I recognised him from your description, but I thought him having a similar sounding ring might be a coincidence. But then George told me the guy's fingerprints were at the murder scene.'

'Who was it?' said Ghita.

'Cracker,' I said. 'But he's only a suspect. There could be many reasons why he went to the dressing room. And it may not be Lance's ring, although it sounded identical.'

'I thought there was something dodgy about him. He looked right into the cash register when he came into the shop,' said Ghita.

'I don't think he'll come back. It's not like we have anything to steal,' I said.

Grace swallowed.

'I'm sorry. What must you think of me? Coming down here and shouting at you?'

'Oh, don't worry. I'm used to it. George shouts at me all the time. Was he polite to you?'

'Actually, he behaved like a gentleman, and not a horrible policeman. He told me he would catch the bad man.'

'George is a good policeman. He'll do his best,' I said. 'I hope you'll forgive me.'

'Of course. But I need more cake.'

'Cake?' said Ghita.

'Your new flavour. I dreamed about it last night. Max says I'm mad, but I need more.'

'I'm sure we can do something about that. Ghita will bake you a whole cake if you want one, won't you?'

'Absolutely. Is that the elderflower and pomegranate one?'

'Yes. It's exquisite,' said Grace. 'I don't think I've ever tasted anything like it before.'

'I can bake one this afternoon and bring it to your shop if you fancy?'

'Sold.'

'We haven't seen you at Fat Fighters for ages,' said Ghita. 'I've got a step class at six this evening. Why don't you come?'

'I'll ring Joy Wells too,' I said. 'She hasn't come for ages. We can all go to the Shanty for a natter afterwards.'

'I'd like that. Don't bother delivering the cake, Ghita. I'll pick it up at the class.'

Chapter 20

We staggered out of Ghita's Fat Fighters club into a warm night and made our separate ways to the Shanty Pub. I gave Grace a lift because Max needed their car to deliver a chest of drawers to the other side of Seacastle. Helen had jumped at the chance to come to one of Ghita's classes and have a glass of wine at the Shanty, but Olivia had turned up her nose and told us she had better things to do. Lance's death had given the remaining competitors a genuine chance to win and Olivia intended to take full advantage. Instead of joining us at Fat Fighters, she called Cindy and Tawny and arranged to meet them at the theatre for some extra rehearsals.

Helen took a dim view of Olivia's idea, which involved her walking there and back by herself at night. Mouse saw his chance and offered to go with her to keep her company. I admired his persistence. Olivia had showed zero interest in him, but he kept trying. Helen had pursed her lips, but agreed as long as Mouse looked out for her. Olivia pouted and sulked, but agreed. I had to hide my amusement, but, in truth, I felt glad Mouse would keep an eye on her. Olivia did not always enjoy Helen's helicopter approach to parenting. I had tried to intervene on occasion, but being told you don't even have children can put you off having an opinion, no matter how many times you've seen the same problem.

The step class had been exhilarating. I had forgotten what fun they could be when everyone turned up. Ghita had put on some disco music and soon we were all panting and laughing and singing along in a breathless way. Even Flo had managed to keep up. Jasmine fitted in with the other ladies and the other new arrivals at the class. Ghita made them stand in the front row so they could follow her steps while we all got hopelessly lost behind them. The disco music thumped out from the speakers and drove us on to the end of the class. I hadn't felt so liberated for ages.

My job at the theatre had proved to be a lot less pleasant than I had anticipated. The murder had only increased the infighting and one-upmanship. Olivia had complained someone had untuned her guitar just before rehearsal. She also told us that Cindy had found a large stain on her stage outfit. Cynthia had offered to remove it, but Cindy didn't trust her either. Tawny had shacked up with Hunter, hoping to protect herself from the unfortunate incidents. She had not revealed why she thought this would work. I envied Jasmine her quick work with their portraits. Now, nobody wanted to be interviewed and I struggled to say anything nice about anyone.

Joy had reserved our usual table tucked into the banquettes at the back of the pub. She asked Shayla to take our order and made us all cheer when she said, 'this one's on the house'. I didn't feel like talking about Lance, but nobody wanted to talk about anything else.

'Tell us about this new suspect,' said Joy.

'You know I can't tell you anything,' said Flo.

'Come on,' said Roz. 'We can't help George if we don't know some inside information.'

'There's nothing new going on. D.I. Antrim has arrested Wayne Dawson, a known burglar and mugger for attacking Grace on the High Street. His finger prints were on the whisky bottle and a glass in Lance's dressing room. D.I. Antrim has basically declared the case closed. We're only tidying up the loose ends according to him.'

Murmurs of sympathy for Grace followed a collective gasp at this revelation, and then we exchanged stories of robbery and loss. Grace shrank under the scrutiny, but she managed to accept the flood of interest without getting cross. I tried to help by dragging the conversation back to Wayne.

'And has Antrim interviewed him yet?' I said. 'I'd love to know how Wayne got hold of the ring.'

'What ring?' said Jasmine.

'The one Frank Sinatra gave to Lance.' I said.

'Frank Sinatra? That must be worth a fortune.'

'He wore it in the photograph you took,' I said.

'That ugly thing? I didn't even notice it.'

She wrote something in a notebook. Flo checked that nobody else in the bar could hear what she was about to say. She shifted to the edge of her seat and lowered her voice to a whisper, forcing us all to lean in to hear her.

'Cracker says Lance gave the ring to him,' she hissed.

'And why would he do that?' said Ghita. 'Unless Cracker threatened him.'

'Who's Cracker?' said Jasmine, who had taken out her pen again.

'This is off the record,' said Joy. 'You can't take notes, or you'll have to leave.'

Jasmine frowned and she took a swig from her drink.

'Why should some other journo get the scoop?' she said. 'I was there when Lance died.'

'You were?' said Roz, raising an eyebrow. 'I'd keep that quiet if I were you.'

Everybody laughed, but Jasmine did not join in. I didn't remember seeing her there. Was there something she hadn't told me?

'Anyway, back to Wayne. Or should I say Cracker. I'm not going to ask how Ghita knows his nickname,' said Flo.

More giggling.

'He's Goose's friend,' said Ghita, crossing her arms. 'He helped clear out the Italian café.'

'He doesn't sound like an animal lover,' said Joy.

'Goose is Mouse's friend,' said Ghita, red in the face with frustration.

'Quite a menagerie,' said Grace. 'And I'm pretty sure I wasn't attacked by a biscuit.'

'Okay, that's enough,' I said, patting Ghita's arm. 'Don't rise to the bait. They're teasing you.'

'It's not my fault Mouse's friends all have silly names,' she said. 'Anyway, why would Lance give Cracker the ring?'

'Cracker says Lance is his grandfather,' said Flo. 'He told the D.I. that he went to see him when his grandmother told him the truth. He says that after the initial shock, Lance relaxed and they had a whisky together. Lance asked him if he'd take the ring and give it to his mother. He asked Cracker to tell her he never knew about her or he would have visited or helped her. Cracker said they shook hands and when he left, Lance was alive.'

'What a load of rubbish,' said Jasmine.

'But who's his mother,' said Roz, who prides herself on knowing everyone's family tree and all their dark and dirty secrets.

'Delia Dawson,' said Flo. 'She lives in the council block behind the hospital.'

'I know her,' said Joy. 'She did some cleaning in here for a while, but I had to let her go.'

She made a sign for drinking with her hand.

'Poor woman,' said Roz. 'What did she do to deserve this?'

'Deserve what?' said Grace, who had zoned out for a while, being unused to our freestyle conversations.

'Somebody dropped Delia off at the local children's home when she was only a few hours old,' said Flo. 'That's what Cracker told D.I. Antrim anyway. Delia found her birth mother a few years ago, and she recently persuaded her to tell her the name of her father.'

'But if Lance fathered Delia, who was her mother?' said Jasmine.

'Cracker wouldn't tell us. He said he'd got his grandfather killed already and he wasn't going to do the same to his grandmother,' said Flo.

'It should be easy enough to find out,' I said. 'But it's unlikely she murdered Lance. Maybe it would be kinder to let her keep her anonymity.'

'But does D.I. Antrim believe in Cracker's innocence?' asked Roz.

'Absolutely not. He's planning on charging him with murder. He says it's an open and shut case,' said Flo.

'But where did Cracker get the scarf?' I said.

'What scarf?' said Joy.

'Somebody drugged Lance and then strangled him with a Brighton and Hove Albion scarf. The problem is that the scarf belonged to Mouse.'

'Did he leave it here?' said Joy.

'I don't know. He had it with him the night we saw Lance perform here at the Shanty, and he couldn't find it afterwards,' I said. 'D.I. Antrim tried to pin the murder on Mouse first.'

Joy's hand flew to her mouth and she emitted a yelp.

'I gave it to her,' said Joy. 'Delia Dawson. She found it in a cupboard and asked me if she could have it. I didn't realise it belonged to Mouse.'

'So, you gave it to her, and she gave it to Cracker, who strangled Lance with it,' said Roz.

'He couldn't have murdered Lance,' said Ghita, shaking her head.

'How do you know,' said Joy.

'He just couldn't,' said Ghita. 'I know Cracker. He's not a bad person. Not really. He wouldn't kill someone for a ring.'

'What if that someone got his grandmother pregnant and ran off to Monte Carlo, leaving her to fend for herself?' I said. 'What if you were burning up with resentment about your mother's hard life, and your grandmother having to give her up?'

'Maybe D.I. Antrim has a point,' said Flo.

'Maybe he does,' I said.

'I don't believe it,' said Ghita. 'I'll never believe it. Cracker's naughty, but he wouldn't kill anyone.'

'I hope you're right,' I said. 'Mouse is not going to take this well. He's fond of Cracker too, and he's usually right about people.'

'He's right this time too,' said Ghita, determined to have the last word.

'Who's seen the new costume drama on the Beeb,' said Joy. 'I'm not sure I like all the bonking.'

I gave her a grateful look.

'I think we need another drink if we're going to talk about bonking,' said Grace. 'My round I think.'

Chapter 21

After I got home, I lay in bed, mulling over the murder of Lance Emerald. I found it hard to belief D.I. Antrim had already declared the case closed. The speed at which he had discovered the murderer spelled almost certain doom for George. The Superintendent, an odious little man who hated George, had been looking for an excuse to replace him, and clearing a murder off the books at this speed would qualify. As much as I struggled with my feelings for George and the way he had treated me, I had learned a thing or two from Harry, about letting bygones be bygones, and behaving like the adult in the room.

I worried about Sharon's reaction to a move or demotion for George, and, to tell the truth, I didn't want him to leave Seacastle. The relationship between Mouse and George had improved so much since George had moved me out, and Mouse had moved in with me. I had also gained a surrogate son and I didn't want him to be hurt by George leaving him again.

I could find no solace in sleep and got up not long after dawn. Stuffing some old toast into my pocket, I wandered down to the beach to sit in my favourite wind shelter and gaze at the wind farm. I hardly ever saw it with the sun coming in from the east, and the view left me awestruck. The sound of the waves breaking on the pebbles made me close my eyes and breathe deeply. I could feel all my stress seeping away with the withdrawing tide. I was halfway to Nirvana when a voice broke through my meditation.

'Can I join you?'

Helen hovered in front of me, tugging at her sleeves. I patted the bench.

'Of course. How did you know I was here?'

'I didn't. I couldn't sleep.'

'Ditto.'

She fluffed out her coat and plumped down on the other end of the bench from me, which made me sad. I sat staring at the sky, wondering what to say. The waves tickled the edge of the pebble bank turning over new treasures for hunters of souvenirs. Helen cleared her throat.

'I'm worried about Olivia.'

I couldn't believe my ears. Had she come to complain about Mouse? My hackles raised.

'Any particular reason?' I said, trying to keep my tone even.

I don't think she noticed. She frowned and wrung her hands.

'This competition is not a healthy environment for her. I don't want to stop her competing. After all, it's her dream, and she's not a little girl anymore.'

Her voice sounded croaky with emotion.

'No, she's not. But I understand why you're concerned.'

Suddenly, she slid along the bench until our thighs were touching. Her plump leg radiated heat through my cold jeans and I held my breath. To my surprise, she took my hand and squeezed it. I could feel tears behind my eyeballs threatening to explode down my cheeks like the water when a lock gate is released.

'I'm so sorry,' she said, sniffing.

'Me too,' I said.

'We used to be such good friends. How come we don't talk anymore? I'd love to be able to pick up the phone and have a natter, like normal sisters.'

I hadn't the heart to remind her how she had behaved when I had depression, or how she took George's side in the divorce. Harry's little sermon about my childish behaviour had penetrated deep. Instead, I squeezed her hand back.

'We can talk now. Did something happen last night?'

'Olivia came back from the theatre all gung-ho, talking about a plan she'd made with the girls to stop the sabotage, and give them a chance of winning the competition. She thinks they can catch whoever it is red-handed, but I'm afraid. What if the murderer hasn't finished yet?'

'But the murderer is in custody. The sabotage is unrelated, as far as I know.'

'So why is D.I. Antrim still stalking the corridors? Olivia says he is lurking in the shadows spying on them all. He has re-interviewed everyone twice.'

'Really? That's odd. I thought Cracker was a shoo-in.'

'Are you sure it's him though, this Cracker fellow? Ghita seemed pretty convinced he didn't do it.'

'Ghita is a little naïve at the best of times. Remember, Cracker mugged Grace. He's no angel.'

'I know, but Ghita seemed so sure. Why would Cracker murder his grandfather for a ring? It doesn't make any sense. Can you help me find out if there's anything going on at the Pavilion?'

'I'll do my best, but I can't antagonise D.I. Antrim. He doesn't need any more ammunition against George.'

'I'm happy you two are getting on again. But...'

'You think the menage-a-trois is a bit weird? Join the crowd. Harry's being tolerant, because of George's troubles. And George is helping Harry find his brother. But I'm in the middle. On the other hand, George is living with Sharon. No matter how well we are getting on, that's the reality. George divorced me, and I'm going out with Harry. Please don't judge me.'

'Who said I was judging you?'

'Nobody. Nobody did. Don't get cross with me. I'm trying to explain what's going on here. Anyway, I'm not the only one in a menage-a-trois. Ghita's in love with a gay couple. It's all the rage.'

I couldn't help grinning and to my relief, Helen grinned back.

'She's a dark horse. I'd never have imagined her in any sort of relationship, never mind one like that. She's so prim.'

'She just needed the right man, or men. Don't tell her you know. She's blissfully happy in her weirdness.'

'I won't. It's great she's happy at last,' she said.

Just then a huge herring gull swooped in and landed at our feet. He swaggered over to us, his tail feathers wagging his whole body to and fro. He planted himself in front of me and cocked his head to one side.

'Oh, my heavens, he's enormous. Look at that beak,' said Helen, cowering. 'Should we shoo him away? Maybe if we both do it, he'll leave us alone.'

'I doubt it. He's part of my harem.'

'Your what?'

'My harem. Three men for one woman is a harem. This is Herbert the herring gull, and he wants something I have in my pocket.'

'Give it to him then, or he might peck us.'

'I doubt it. He's all feathers and no beak.'

I pulled the toast out of my pocket and tossed it to him. He threw back his head and screamed in glee. Then he picked both slices up with his bright yellow beak and scampered off down the promenade. He unfolded his wings and took off, leaving us both breathless in admiration.

'Herbert?' said Helen.

'The herring gull. I've been feeding him since he was a juvenile. Isn't he cute?'

'Enormous is the word you are looking for. And terrifying. Only you would call him cute.'

'Do you want some breakfast?'

'I'm starving.'

'Let's have boiled eggs and raise a spoon to Daddy.'

'Now you've made me tearful again.'

'It's that kind of day.'

Chapter 22

After Helen left, I drove to Second Home. I had to park so far away; it would have been quicker to walk. I patted the bonnet of the Mini and left her in the sunshine. When I got to the shop, I noticed several large streaks down the window, indicating enraged herring gull syndrome had struck again. They always squirted their faeces at the windows when they were clean. I presumed they were reacting to seeing their reflection in the glass. Maybe they thought their reflection could be a rival gull? All I know is that every single time I cleaned the windows, the gulls immediately made them dirty again. If I left the streaks, people couldn't see the furniture displayed in the window. I never found it less than annoying.

I ran the water in the sink and put on some rubber gloves. The cleaning cloth had more holes than a crochet doily, but I rinsed it and took it out to clean the worst of the dirt off the glass. The faeces had dried hard, but it couldn't resist my firm intent to dislodge it. Then, I ditched the cloth in the bin and came back outside with my vinegar spray bottle and some brown paper. I rubbed the window clean, knowing it wouldn't be long before some nutty gull launched another attack. As I picked the used pieces of brown paper off the ground, I became aware of a pair of tiny feet in ballet pumps standing in front of me. I straightened up to find Marge from the hairdresser planted there, her hair wild and mascara streaks on her cheeks. I almost leant forward to remove them with my trusty vinegared paper.

'Marge?'

'You must help me. I'm so desperate. I don't know what to do.'

'We can't talk here. Will you come in and have a cup of tea or coffee with me?'

She looked around as if checking for someone following her.

'Are you sure no one will hear us?'

'I'm pretty sure. I'll lock the door if you want.'

'Okay. Thank you. I'd love a cup of tea.'

'If you need a sugar boost, I can offer you some lemon and lime drizzle cake with cardamom.'

'Is it nice?'

'It's beyond delicious.'

'Okay.'

I closed the door behind us and left the closed sign up. Marge heaved herself slowly up the stairs, wincing, and I wondered how old she was. Perhaps all that dancing had worn out her joints? Or maybe a dodgy hip? I followed her up and turned on the coffee machine. I cut her a slice of cake and put it on a plate for her. She sat on the bench opposite the machine, her thin legs swinging. I gave her the cake and a small fork and started to make us a pot of strong tea. She poked the cake with her fork and separated a smidgen to taste. I heard a yelp of approval as I filled the tea pot with boiling water and smirked. When I came over with the tray, she had almost polished off the slice and she was using her finger to gather up the remains of the icing on the plate.

'Feeling better after the sugar boost?' I said.

'Yes, thanks. Sorry to disturb you in the middle of washing the windows, but I needed to speak to you urgently.'

She looked at her plate again as if searching for something to say, or more cake, I couldn't tell which.

'I need your help,' she said. 'My grandson's been arrested for murder.'

My astonishment was tempered by the sensation of more pieces of the jigsaw sliding into place.

'What's his name? I asked, though I knew.

'Wayne Dawson. Most people know him as Cracker.'

'Is this the Lance Emerald murder?'

'Yes, but he didn't do it. It's my fault you see. I told him to go there.'

'You did? I don't understand.'

'His mother Delia is my daughter, Lance's daughter.'

'You got pregnant while you toured with the Balentines?'

'Yes, but I never told anyone, not even Lance. I was going out with Reg at the time, and I simply couldn't tell him. He might have killed Lance, if he found out. I left the shows and hid with an aunt here in Seacastle until the birth, because being an unmarried mother was a massive cause of shame in those days.'

'What happened to Delia afterwards? It must have been hard bringing her up.'

'My family would never have let me ruin my life like that. They told me she died at birth from a heart issue. In those days you weren't allowed to see the baby, because it was thought too distressing for the mother, so I believed them. But they had lied to me and left her at the children's home.'

'How did you find out that Delia is your baby?'

'She contacted me about six months ago. I didn't believe her at first, but she showed me the paperwork. It shocked me to the core, but I've never been so happy. It's worn off a little since I realised how damaged she is, but she's my little girl and I love her. I asked her not to tell Wayne about me yet, because I'd heard about him and he frightened me.'

'Because he's a petty criminal?'

'Yes. Delia agreed to keep my secret if I told her the name of her father.'

'Wow! She must have been surprised.'

'That's putting it mildly. I meant to explain things to Wayne as well eventually, but I didn't get the chance. He spotted some photographs when he cleaned out the old Italian café. He saw a dancer who looked identical to Delia. He put two and two together. He's an impetuous lad, but not violent. So Delia told him I was his grandmother. He came to see me and demanded to know everything about Lance. I told him some of it. Enough to make him want to meet his grandfather.'

'Do you know why he went?'

'He wanted a proper family. Delia has always been a chaotic mother. I think he wanted something better. God knows I tried to warn him about Lance.'

'The police think he killed Lance to steal his ring.'

'The one he claims to have received from Frank Sinatra?'

'The gold one with the large purple garnet.'

Marge shook her head.

'He did get a ring from Frank, but he gave it to a hooker in Blackpool when he was drunk and wanted sex with her. The ring you just described was mine. Lance stole it from me when we had our fling. It belonged to my grandmother. Wayne went to ask for it to be returned. I think Lance gave it to him for me. Lance wasn't all bad. I know he regretted what happened between us.'

'How do you know that?'

'He wrote to me. And he let me know he'd be coming home too. I think he planned to look me up.'

'I'm sorry there was no happy ending for you two.'

She shrugged.

'I guess I'll have to wait till we both end up in hell. But I want to do right by my grandson. There's no way he murdered Lance. No way.'

She crossed her arms and pursed her lips in a stubborn line.

'What do you want me to do about it?'

'I want you to investigate the murder. I can pay.'

Who did she think I was? Columbo?

'I'm not a private detective. I run a vintage shop.'

'But you were an investigative reporter on that show. What was it called?'

'Uncovering the Truth.'

'That's it. You were amazing.'

'I appeared for only five minutes an episode.'

'But you were the brains of the show. Everybody knows that. The other presenters were just talking heads.'

I'm susceptible to flattery. I don't get much attention and it isn't always positive, but when someone praises the fruits of my career, my judgement tends to go out of the window. I beamed.

'Look, I'll give it a try, but it's a little delicate. Also, the forensics are pointing at Wayne so I don't know how much use I'll be.'

She started to fumble with the clasp on her handbag, but I put my hand over it.

'I've got savings,' she said. 'I'm not a charity.'

'You don't need to pay me. My niece and stepson are embroiled in this affair. And my ex-husband. That's reason enough for me to get involved. But I'll need your help.'

'I won't talk to the police.'

'It's not up to me. I can't stop them questioning you. D.I. Antrim is not likely to listen to me while I'm still on his suspect list.'

'How can I help?'

'I need to speak to Delia. She may hold the key to this investigation.'

Marge sighed.

'She's not often sober. My girl's had a tough life.'

'What if I ask her to come and clean the shop?'

'That might work. She won't drink if she has a cleaning job. She needs the money.'

'Can you ask her then? And let me know when she can come?'

'I'll do my best. Seeing as you won't accept cash, maybe I could give you a nice cut and blow-dry sometime?'

'Now we're talking.'

After Marge had left the shop, I mulled over the facts as I knew them. Lance had been murdered in his dressing room. Someone had drugged and strangled him. The method of murder indicated a squeamishness which suggested the murderer had wanted to kill Lance without having to struggle with him. George would have called it a soft murder. He often let his stone age attitudes invade his investigations, but I felt he might be right this time. It seemed like the act of someone who cared about Lance, or at least didn't want him to know who killed him.

The list of suspects had just got longer, and something Marge had said had stuck in my mind, that she had told Cracker 'some of the story'. Alarm bells rang as I considered this statement. What hadn't she told him? Who else might have something to lose or a reason for revenge if they found out about Marge's pregnancy? And Lance's death had cleared the path for ambitious tributes like Hunter and Cindy to rise to the top. I needed to question Cynthia now I knew about her past. Could she have a reason to murder Lance if she found out about Marge's baby? And then there was Reg, solid lovable Reg, who used to be handsome and snake-hipped. I'd place a large bet Lance wasn't the only man who had an easy time seducing young women. Luckily, I still had the excuse of finishing the interviews, and now I had been hired to investigate, I had my own motives for finding out the truth.

Chapter 23

I returned to the Pavilion with a certain amount of trepidation in case I bumped into D.I. Antrim. I had the feeling he would extract all my secrets with little more than a steely glare. In another life, I would have found him quite attractive, but I would have fattened him up a bit. I could imagine all those bones sticking into me in bed. Ouch. I shook my head to remove all visions of D.I. Antrim without his customary grey suit and shiny brogues. If he had appeared in an Agatha Christie movie, I wouldn't have blinked an eye.

My choice of who to interview first did not depend on me. As I entered through the stage door and up the stairs to the corridor, Cindy grabbed my arm and pulled me into one of the dressing rooms. It had a glamour not seen in either of the men's rooms I had seen. The pink walls reflected in four large make up mirrors with the customary light bulb surround.

Tawny sat at one of them screwing up her face as she attempted to pluck one of the few eyebrow hairs she had left. Her long acrylic nails tapped on the mirror as she leaned in to focus. She looked me up and down in the reflection and she smirked at my jeans and sweatshirt. I could tell she disapproved of my outfit. I had dressed for comfort as I had intended to stay at the shop. She wore a gold Lycra dress which hugged her every curve and a pair of vertiginous nude heels. Cindy's ensemble consisted of a tutu and strappy crop-top. Both outfits struck me as a little over the top, but I know I'm old fashioned. It's hard to ignore the rules you were taught as a child. I tried to curb my judgemental streak and enjoy their freedom to wear anything they wanted. Like I could, if I got past my upbringing.

'You look nice,' I said. 'What's the big secret, Cindy?'

Cindy glanced at Tawny for approval and Tawny gave an almost imperceptible nod.

'D.I. Antrim arrested some random bloke for Lance's murder,' she said.

I nearly told them Cracker was far from random, but I decided to absorb information rather than share it. I didn't know how these two were involved, if at all. Cindy chewed manically on a piece of gum, twisting it with her tongue and blowing bubbles. She seemed unable to sit down, rather pacing between the row of mirrors and the pink sofas.

'I had heard. My ex is a policeman, you know,' I said.

The wrong thing to say. They exchanged panicked glances. I regrouped.

'I said ex. I'd rather die than tell him anything to help in the investigation.'

'Cynthia says you worked in that show; Uncovering the Truth,' said Tawny swinging her chair around.

'I did the research for the programme for seven years,' I said.

'Have you got any contacts in television?' said Cindy. 'Only, I, we, could do with a break.'

'I'm afraid not. Documentary and Drama do not often have crew in common.'

'I told you,' said Tawny. 'She can't help us.'

'But do you know why Lance got his self killed?' said Cindy. 'It weren't the ring, if that's what they told you. Nobody believed his story about Frank Sinatra.'

Tawny put her finger to her lips. Again, their complicity intrigued me.

'No, but I'm intending on doing my own investigation. You may have information that is relevant to the inquiry without knowing it. For instance, I understand that somebody sabotaged your dress. Did you find out who did it, or why?'

Cindy turned pale and backed into a chair shaking her head.

'No, I didn't.'

'Did you identify the substance which stained your dress?'

'No, but it smelled funny and left a purple stain. Cynthia couldn't get it out. I had to borrow something else to wear from wardrobe.'

'Your new dress is much nicer,' said Tawny. 'Much, much nicer.'

There was something in the way she said it that made me wonder if she had sabotaged Cindy's dress and felt guilty about it.

'Lance liked my other one.'

'Lance is dead, sweety. He didn't always have everyone's best interest at heart. Why don't you go and make us a cup of tea? Tanya needs to interview me, and it might as well be now.'

'Okay. Back soon.'

Cindy wiggled her way out of the room and I had a vision of Marilyn Monroe on the station platform in Some Like It Hot. She had the same blonde hair and exaggerated hourglass figure, and I had a feeling she also had Marilyn's sharp intellect hidden under that dumb act. I had deliberately used uncommon words when speaking to her, but she hadn't noticed.

I sat in the chair next to Tawny and crossed my legs.

'Have you always wanted to be on the stage?'

'Pretty much. I used to stay in my room singing along to Spotify with my hairbrush.'

'Why did you stick around? This tribute show is old news. You could make it big anywhere else.'

'I'm not sure. Misplaced loyalty perhaps. I love my fellow competitors. We're all a little damaged and that gives us kinship.'

'Is that why Olivia doesn't fit in?'

Tawny sneered.

'She's too pure. Imagine doing the singer/songwriter thing in this day and age. Who does she think she is? Ed Sheeran?'

'But with Lance gone, doesn't she have the same chance everybody has?'

'I thought you were supposed to be smart. This competition is more rigged than a schooner.'

'But with Lance dead, doesn't that change the game?'

'You'll need to ask Cynthia that. She calls the show, and I've heard she calls the shots too.'

I looked up from my notebook to catch a wretched look on her face.

'I guess you have to spend a lot of time away from your family doing these shows,' I said. 'That must be hard.'

'I don't have a family,' she said. 'My mother was too busy to look after children. She gave me away to her sister.'

I didn't know how to respond to this piece of news. I played for time by pretending to cross something out and rewrite it.

'It's okay,' she said. 'I'm so over it. I have another family now, in this show. Cynthia is our mother, and Lance is our drunken father. Was, I meant was.'

'Not much of a father,' I said. 'Did he ever make a pass at you?'

'Lance made a pass at everyone, even Olivia.'

'Olivia? She didn't tell me that.'

'She's a dark horse, our girl. She likes to meet someone in the storage room. Who knows what goes on there?'

I couldn't tell if she had invented this piece of gossip. Did she know I was Olivia's aunt? Or was she just being malicious out of habit? I didn't have time to find out. Cindy backed into the room carrying a tray with three mugs of tea.

'I put milk in already,' she said. 'Do you take sugar?'

'No sugar, thank you,' I said. 'How long have you known each other?'

'All our lives,' said Tawny, before Cindy could answer.

'Sure feels like it,' said Cindy.

I laughed at her drole tone, but Tawny pursed her lips.

'Nothing is as it seems around here,' she said. 'Everyone's acting, don't forget. Anyone could have killed Lance.'

'Cherché la femme,' said Cindy.

Definitely not a dumb blonde.

Chapter 24

I decided to drop in on Reg at the Pavilion. He had managed to stay out of the spotlight so far, lurking in his room, trying to firefight the haemorrhaging ticket sales. Mouse had been banished, due to Reg's agitation. I suspected Mouse felt relieved, as Reg could get hysterical under stress. A murder at the theatre should have increased the interest in the show, but the target audience were jaded. People had tolerated the fixed nature of the results for years, like they did at the wrestling, but it had lost its gloss as a result. The show did not qualify as a competition, but as an entertainment, and with Lance winning every show, people had become bored. I had not appreciated this before, but now I could see how it would affect the stakes for the rest of the cast. If they knew they couldn't win, but they got paid anyway, did that remove or increase their desire to get rid of Lance? And who would murder someone to compete in a rigged competition? Killing Lance did not guarantee success.

I knocked on the door of Reg's office and heard him ask me in. When I entered his face lit up and he bustled over to me. Behind him it looked as if a bomb had gone off. Piles of paper teetered beside an ancient Dell computer. A tattered mouse mat with a lighthouse design sat under a greasy looking mouse which added to the great ball of tangled cables on his desk. I wondered how he tolerated such a mess. It didn't fit his fastidious image at all. No wonder Mouse had taken his rejection without protest. Reg cleared a stack of brochures from the seat of a chair and indicated I should sit on it. He plonked himself down in his own and swivelled towards me rubbing his hands together.

'You're still here. That's great. I guess being married to the Bill makes you immune to the horrors of murder.'

'I wouldn't say that. Lance's death shocked me. It seemed so unfair considering his illness.'

Reg blinked.

'What illness? Unless you mean groping sickness. He certainly had that in spades.'

I reached out to put my hand on his arm.

'Lance had terminal cancer. Didn't you know?'

He grabbed his arm back, his eyes wide.

'Cancer? Who told you that?'

'He did. When I interviewed him. He asked me not to tell anyone, but I don't expect it matters anymore.'

Reg opened his mouth to speak, but seemed paralysed with shock.

'But I would never have... If I had only known. Oh dear.'

'You would never have what?' I asked.

'I can't... It's just that we went way back together.'

'You were in the Balentines together, weren't you.'

'That's right. How did you know?'

'I spoke to an old friend of yours.'

I scrolled through my files and handed him my phone with the photograph Marge had given me of herself and Cynthia on the screen. He stared at it for ages without saying anything. A short gasp escaped him and he increased the magnification as he examined first one and then the other of the double act.

'Has Cynthia seen this?' he said. 'It's amazing. I don't remember this photograph. It seems like our partnership only happened yesterday.'

He caressed the image on the screen with his thumb, but I couldn't see which of the women provoked this show of affection. Then he opened his desk drawer and took out an old photograph of Lance and him on stage as the Balentines.

'You realise that slim fellow with hair is me?' he said. 'I'm unrecognisable now, I'm afraid. Time waits for no man.'

'Of course I recognised you,' I said, lying valiantly. 'You haven't changed a bit.'

Reg grinned.

'Well, that's true at least. I've haven't changed a bit; I've changed a lot.'

He barked out a short, fake laugh.

'May I make a copy with my phone? I might use it in an article.'

'Sure. I doubt it's under copyright after all this time.'

I took out my phone and snapped a copy, taking care to get the whole thing in the frame. I put the phone back in my handbag.

'You must have been disappointed when Lance left the act. Was it weird for you, him coming back to town after so long away?'

Reg took so long to answer that I became uneasy. Perhaps he still harboured resentment and didn't appreciate me coming to remind him of it? He swallowed and cleared his throat.

'When Lance took off, I missed him more than I can say. We were like peas and carrots. Bing Crosby and Fred Astaire. I couldn't believe he'd desert me like that. I kept hoping he'd turn up like a bad penny and take up where we left off. The worst thing was not hearing from him. Not a single phone call or a postcard. Nothing.'

'That's awful,' I said. 'You must have been devastated.'

'Of course. I lost my living too. Nobody could replace Lance. He had a fabulous voice and buckets of charm. The audiences loved him. I didn't have his charisma. Without Lance, I was toast on the circuit.'

'But you took over the management of the Pavilion not so long afterwards, didn't you?'

'That's right. I fell on my feet, thank goodness. An old patron of our shows bought the Pavilion when it had almost collapsed into disrepair. I project managed its restoration for him and stayed on to run it afterwards. I've been here ever since.'

'Do you ever see Marge?'

His face fell.

'No. Not since she left me too. At the same time as Lance. I guess it wasn't fun anymore once he had gone. Lance ran the party. Once he left, the fun petered out and Marge dumped me. I don't blame her; I couldn't raise a smile for months. She broke my heart by leaving me, and I haven't ever recovered.'

'Isn't it hard living in Seacastle, knowing how close she is?'

'Not really. She stays out of my way, and to tell you the truth, I don't mind knowing she's nearby.'

'I guess Lance coming home must have upset the apple cart?'

He shrugged.

'In the beginning, I couldn't wait to see him again. Stupid man that I am. I intended to let bygones be bygones and renew our friendship.'

'But you were disappointed?'

'I can't tell you how much. And then…'

I waited, but he shook his head.

'And then what?'

'Water under the bridge now. Lance is dead. He brought it on himself.'

He crossed his arms.

'I know this is going to sound odd, with all the vitriol flying around about Lance, but I liked him,' I said.

He looked at me with pity in his eyes.

'Everyone liked Lance in the beginning. He was a skilled capturer of hearts. It's what he did next that counted. Why do you think we all hate him now?'

Chapter 25

I breathed in a few large lungfuls of sea air on the promenade before I walked back to the Mini to drive home. The sun was already lurking low in the west reminding me the nights would soon be drawing in, and the Indian summer over. The few tourists intrepid enough to come to Seacastle had dwindled to a trickle of pensioners looking for special rates on their fish and chips. I wondered how Harry had fared in his search for Nick. His absence left a large hole at the Grotty Hovel. To make things worse, Mouse spend most of his time next door with the traitor Hades, leaving me bereft and grumpy. My finger hovered over Helen's number as I contemplated calling her and inviting her over for supper.

The phone rang in my hand giving me a fright and almost causing me to drop it on the pavement. Mouse had bought me a shock proof cover after realising I couldn't be trusted with such a delicate piece of modern technology. I puffed my cheeks out in relief and held it to my ear.

'Tan? Is that you?'

Helen. We must be psychic sisters.

'Yes, I just finished at the Pavilion. I planned on a quick visit to the supermarket on the way home. Do you want to come to my house for supper?'

'Oh, no, yes, I would, but Martin just called and asked me to come home for the weekend. I thought you might keep an eye on Olivia for me?'

'No problem. Tell her to come over for supper. I'll buy something nice.'

'Great. See you Monday.'

Martin, Helen's phantom husband, provided everything she ever wanted. The comfortable middle-class life with a beautiful talented daughter and no money worries. In my experience, it was unlike him to summon her anywhere. It usually worked the other way around as he embodied self-effacement when I saw him. However, I could take advantage of the situation to quiz Olivia on her love life and to ask her what she was doing the day of Lance's murder, so I had no complaints.

'Have a nice weekend.'

I bought fresh salmon fillets and some broccoli and new potatoes for supper. Simple and delicious. Mouse grinned in appreciation as I unpacked the food.

'Yum. What's the occasion?'

'Your cousin is coming to supper. Helen had to go back to Martin for the weekend.'

'She's not my cousin. She's...'

'Hm. I don't think she's that either. Listen, can you do me a favour and make yourself scarce after we eat. Pretend you have something important to do on your computer upstairs.'

'But I finally get the chance to talk to her alone without her chaperone.'

'That's what I want to do. I think she's hiding something from me about Lance's murder.'

'Why can't I be there?'

'Because Cindy told me Olivia has been seeing Hunter backstage and I need to find out what really happened on the day of Lance's murder.'

His face fell.

'What sort of seeing?'

'I don't know yet. But I doubt she'll answer truthfully with you listening.'

He shrugged.

'No wonder she doesn't laugh at my jokes. Even my best ones.'

'I do.'

He rolled his eyes.

'You have to. It's compulsory.'

The new potatoes were ready to cook and I tossed them into a pan of boiling water with a pinch of salt. After ten minutes, I squeezed some lemon juice onto the salmon fillets and sealed them into foil with a knob of butter. They went into the oven with steam holes poked into the foil. I poured myself and Mouse a glass of Chardonnay each and he texted Olivia to come over for supper.

Five minutes later, she knocked on the front door with Hades in her arms. I found this habit alarming, but he seemed calm enough. I couldn't imagine what I would do if he took fright and jumped in front of a car. The little maggot didn't even acknowledge me and made a beeline for Mouse. Olivia laughed.

'He does it on purpose, you know. The trick is to ignore him. He can't bear that. He thinks he's the most important person in the room.'

She had a point. I returned to the kitchen and poured her a glass of wine. Then we served up and carried the delicious fish and veg out to the table with a jar of dill sauce. Nobody spoke as we ate the delicious fare. Afterwards, we picked at a bowl of strawberries and blueberries as Olivia regaled us with exaggerated anecdotes from backstage at the Pavilion. I wondered if her mother knew what a consummate liar she had become. I caught Mouse's eye and he stood up.

'Damn. I forgot. I have to finish something on the computer. You carry on, I'll be down again shortly. But don't talk about me while I'm away.'

'I'm afraid I can't promise. You'll just have to sit upstairs with your ears burning.'

I refilled Olivia's glass and pointed at the sofa. She smiled and joined me there. Hades immediately sat on her lap, but I pretended not to notice his over-the-top purring and stretching. I took out my notebook and Olivia sighed.

'Really,' she said. 'We're going to do this now? I thought I gave you enough material for the article already.'

'You did. This is about the murder.'

She stiffened, frightening Hades who sprang for his laundry basket, knocking over her glass of wine. I reached behind the sofa and grabbed a handful of paper napkins from the table. We dabbed the pool of wine and managed to soak up most of it. I cursed my luck, knowing I had given her time to get her story straight in her head. Her pale face spoke volumes about the inner turmoil, so I pressed on with my plan.

'More specifically, what you were doing the time of Lance's murder. I saw you coming up from the storage area looking tearful and dishevelled. What were you doing down there?'

'Nothing. I needed to get something, that's all.'

'Did Hunter also need to be there with you, or was that a coincidence?'

Her mouth fell open.

'How did you know? You can't have seen him. He left by the other stairway.'

'I didn't know. But I do now.'

'Who told you about us? It must have been one of the girls. They were so jealous. Cindy warned me off, but I didn't listen to her. Hunter is just like his father.'

Now it was my turn to be confused.

'His father?'

'You didn't know? Lance was Hunter's father. At least that's what Hunter believed.'

'And who is his mother?'

'It's a secret. I can't tell you.'

'You can tell me, or you can tell D.I. Antrim.'

Olivia shook her head.

'You wouldn't. You're my auntie.'

'I lived with a policeman for almost ten years. It's in the blood. I can't lie.'

Except that I lied right then. She didn't know that.

'Cynthia. Okay? Cynthia is his mother. She wouldn't confirm the identity of his father. But he thinks it had to be Lance. Cynthia had an affair with Lance, you know.'

'Yes, I discovered that, but isn't Hunter a little young to be their son?'

She smirked.

'Hunter is a cyborg. He's had more plastic surgery than Cher. He looks twenty years younger than he is. If you look closely, you can spot the scars. And he has regular Botox injections, that's why his face is so blank all the time.'

'You need to tell me what happened that day. It's important.'

Olivia sighed.

'Okay, but don't tell Mum, whatever you do. She's, um, sheltered.'

I snorted with laughter at this description. Daughters are not often aware their mother's had a sex life before they got married. Helen had not been promiscuous, but we grew up with the pill. She had her fair share of boyfriends and heartbreaks. I should know. I helped her through all of them.

'I won't tell her anything, but you may have to talk to George about this or give a statement down at the station, if it's material to the case.'

'I can't believe this is happening to me. I haven't done anything wrong. You might not have noticed, but Hunter is seriously attractive. He has an older man's charm with a younger man's face, and he can sing as well as anyone out there.'

'Oh, I noticed. I'm not dead yet.'

'Well, he flirted with me a few times and made it clear he wanted to hang out together. I tried to ignore him, but it's hard to turn someone like that down. Imagine Brad Pitt flirted with you?'

'I'd rather not. I'm trying to concentrate.'

'Anyway, he suggested we meet downstairs in the dimmer room.'

'Where's that?'

'It's at the back of the storage space. It's where the controls for the lights and other stuff are located. Beside the COSSH cupboard.'

'And what's that?'

'The place they keep the dangerous chemicals that have to be locked up. It's an acronym. I think it stands for chemicals hazardous to health or something like that.'

'What happened down there? Walk me through it.'

Olivia looked away from me and pursed her lips. I waited for her to control her emotions. Hades stuck his face in hers and rubbed against it. She put her arms around him and took a deep breath.

'I went downstairs to the dimmer room about five minutes late, because I had to wait until Jasmine left the basement.'

'What was Jasmine doing down there?'

'I'm not sure. I think Cindy had a stain in her costume that needed removing. She probably got something from the COSSH cupboard'

'And then?'

'Hunter grabbed my arm and pulled me into the room. He said he wasn't used to waiting and he pushed me against the wall. I tried to make a joke and tell him I had expected something romantic, but he started to put his hands under my jumper. He kissed me and forced my mouth open and I bit his tongue. He tried to pull off my top and I got cross and fought back. I managed to escape and came running up the stairs. That's when you saw me.'

'Did you notice anything odd about him?'

'Besides the assault? He seemed hyper. Hunter is always calm. I thought it might be because he felt angry at waiting.'

'Do you think he had been talking to Jasmine before you arrived?'

'Maybe. There isn't much space down there. If she went to the COSSH cupboard, she couldn't have avoided him.'

After Olivia left, I sat on the sofa ignoring Hades who had stayed with me. I didn't feel any closer to identifying the murderer. I had suspects a-plenty, but no-one stuck out. Out of the foursome of elders, every one of them could have had a motive to kill Lance. He had left carnage behind when he disappeared. Ruined careers and broken hearts. But the younger generation also had good reasons to get rid of the old lecher. I needed a catalyst to spark my brain into action. I also needed to chat with George. The murder team should be dispatched to check out the basement and fingerprint the dimmer room.

Chapter 26

Despite my offer of an early coffee at the Vintage, George asked himself to breakfast at the Grotty Hovel. Mouse had not yet stirred, and Hades had made himself comfortable on Mouse's pillow when I looked in on them. I shut the door to prevent Hades coming downstairs. George did not seem to have realised that Hades had become a permanent fixture at the house, although he wouldn't have been much of a detective to pick up on the clues. Hades had shed his fur all over the house and even I had begun to sneeze occasionally when a hair went up my nose.

George had sounded so miserable on the call that I abandoned the idea of serving him a healthy boiled egg and opened a packet of bacon. I lined it on the grill to make us bacon sandwiches for breakfast. I made a strong pot of tea and waited for him to arrive. I also left the front door open so he could come in without ringing the doorbell and waking Mouse and Hades. He pushed it open before eight, and I put my finger to my lips so he would shut it quietly. Being George, he got his signals crossed and grinned at me.

'Have you prepared a romantic breakfast for two?' he said.

'It's too early for romance. I was trying to avoid a father-son face off before I had a chance to eat.'

'Oh. What's cooking?'

'I'm about to put on the bacon for some butties. Do you approve?'

His face lit up.

'Approve? I'm already salivating. Sharon won't let me eat bacon. She says it will give me cancer.'

'It does, if you eat enough. But I think we're safe with a couple of slices each.'

'She's so wrapped up in her new business I hardly see her these days. I'm feeling neglected.'

'Why don't you woo her a little?'

'What do you mean?'

'You know. Book dinner at a fancy restaurant. Buy her flowers. She's not as tolerant as I was. You need to make more effort.'

'She hasn't even asked me about D.I. Antrim pushing in on my territory. Sometimes I think she doesn't care.'

'Give her a chance. She's setting up a new business. That takes twenty-four hours a day in the beginning, you know.'

'Why do you have to be so reasonable? Have you got any brown sauce?'

'Yes, your son prefers it to ketchup.'

'He's got good taste, like his father.'

'And yet he prefers me.'

George's face turned sulky.

'Do we have to talk about that?' he said.

I repented.

'No. I'd rather fill you in on the case. Let me cook the bacon and we can get started.'

As we munched the sandwiches, I observed my ex-husband's ecstatic expression and felt nostalgic. Was ever a man so easy to please as George Carter? I hoped he and Sharon could get past their bump in the road. I had once imagined we could be friends, but the more I found out about her the less likely it became. Only one thing interested her; money and lots of it. She sounded like a right cow, to be honest. Poor George.

'Have you got any new leads? D.I. Antrim is frantic as he can't pin the murder on Wayne Dawson. The little maggot is sticking to his story and there is none of his DNA on the scarf.'

'Whose is?'

'Whose is what?'

'Whose DNA is on the scarf?'

'Oh, we haven't matched most of the samples yet. We're still working on it.'

'You can add Delia Dawson to your list of cross-checks. Delia definitely had the scarf for a while. She may even have used it.'

'Cracker's mother? Where did she get it?'

'Joy Wells gave it to her after Mouse left it in the pub.'

'But if Cracker didn't touch it, how did it find its way around Lance Emerald's neck?' said George.

'Ah. That is the sixty-four-thousand-dollar question. I'm hoping to question Delia tomorrow. She's coming to the Vintage to do some cleaning, so I'll see if I can winkle anything out of her.'

'Anything else?'

'You need to suggest a search of the storage room and the rest of the under-stage area at the Pavilion. I heard from one of the cast, that both Hunter Norman and Jasmine Smith were in or near the dimmer room around the time of the murder.'

'Why is that significant?'

'Do you remember someone had turned the central heating up high and Lance's dressing room was like a sauna?'

'Yes, Flo nearly fainted.'

'Well, the controls for the heating are in the dimmer room. And that's not all.'

'Go on.'

'The COSSH cupboard is there too. What if they kept the Rohypnol hidden in there instead of it being brought in by Cracker. That boy doesn't have the brains to plan a murder. He could have killed Lance in a moment of temper, but I doubt he even knows what Rohypnol can do to a human.'

'That's true. He's no criminal mastermind. He still had Grace's wallet on him.'

'Will he go to prison?'

'Grace refuses to charge him, so we'll have to release him today.'

'That's good news. I hope Delia doesn't realise I'm the one who shopped her son to the police.'

'Cracker's got a record as long as your arm. I don't think it surprised her to hear he got locked up again.'

'Do you have any hunches about the murderer? There seem to be many people with opportunity that day, but I can't find any motives yet.'

'Would you like me to show you some photographs of the main players as I see them?'

'Load up the teapot.'

After George had seen the photographs and taken notes on the motives and counter motives I had extracted from the four entertainers, he sat back on the sofa and shook his head.

'The problem with entertainers is their ability to tell you a lie with a straight face,' he said. 'This is not going to be easy. Let me know if you find anything else.

'Before you go…'

'What?'

'Look, I know you're helping Harry find his brother Nick. Is there anything you can tell me? Harry has gone very quiet.'

'Hasn't he told you? I found Nick in Devon, living in the countryside. Harry went to see him.'

'When?'

'A few days ago. Hasn't he called you?'

'No, he hasn't. I'm sure he has his reasons.'

'They have a lot to sort out. I'm sure he'll tell you when he can. I don't want to break his confidence though.'

'I understand. Thank you George.'

'Chin up, Tan. He'll be back.'

Chapter 27

Delia Dawson could have stepped out of the old photograph of the tramps shown to me by Marge. She had Marge's petite figure and tiny feet, and her cornflower blue eyes in a heart shaped face. Unfortunately, a lifetime of smoking had lined and wrinkled the skin on her face and her hair had that nicotine colour streaking the platinum blonde of her home-dyed hair. In fact, she looked closer in age to the Marge working at the hairdresser's than the one in the photograph. It shocked me to realise she and Hunter were probably the same age. When she spoke, several teeth were either blackened or missing, which made me feel dreadful for her. Her tough life had been etched on her features in a way impossible to ignore.

'You must be Tanya,' she said.' Marge told me you needed cleaning done. You've certainly got a lot of furniture to polish.'

She looked around and ran her hand over one of the table tops inspecting it for dust. She wrinkled her nose in disapproval.

'Is there any call for this old furniture around here?' she said.

I laughed inwardly at myself. We all have opinions of other people's places in life. She obviously thought I sold junk, and felt sorry for me. Harry would have enjoyed the joke. He had treated all old furniture as scrap before he met me. When he saw some of it through my eyes, he had voiced astonishment.

'One man's trash is another man's treasure,' I said. 'You'd be surprised.'

'Where do you want me to start?'

'Why don't you start at the back of the ground floor and work your way upstairs. When you are finished, I'll make you a coffee and pay you. How does that sound?'

Delia did not answer me. She grunted and picked up the bucket of supplies I had provided for her. I watched her for a while, but I could sense her resentment at being monitored, so I went upstairs and wrote a list of my main suspects for the murder. Cracker had been released on bail by D.I. Antrim, but he hadn't featured high up my list of suspects. He did not strike me as having the cold-blooded intelligence necessary to drug Lance and plant Mouse's scarf on the body after using it to strangle him. And anyway, his DNA had not been found on the scarf. Could he have used gloves? His prints on the whisky bottle and the glasses seemed to me to corroborate his version of the story. This also narrowed down the time period when the whisky could have been spiked with Rohypnol. I made a note to ask Delia about the scarf and sucked the end of my pen. Who else could have had a strong enough motive to murder Lance? Nearly everyone.

After my talk with Olivia, Hunter had entered into the frame. I remembered his shock at hearing of Lance's terminal diagnosis. Had he killed Lance in his anxiety to be the top dog without knowing that nature would soon give him a helping hand? If he had suspected Lance of being his father, he might have killed him out of resentment. And what was he doing in the dimmer room before Olivia got there? Cynthia had talked about the central heating being controlled in the basement. Had he used Olivia as a pretext in case anyone else found him there? And last in the frame could be Reg. Marge was the love of his life. If he had found out that Lance had made her pregnant, causing her to run away without telling him, would he have taken revenge? Lance had disappointed him again by not renewing their friendship. Had Reg decided enough was enough?

Delia came upstairs, her face red with exertion, her bucket bouncing off the bannisters.

'Blimey, that took me longer than I thought. I've run out of Pledge too.'

She plonked the bucket on the floor.

'I'm gasping for that coffee now. Can I smoke in here?'

'What type would you like? I'm afraid you can't have a cigarette. The soft furnishings absorb the smell and then I can't sell them.'

She frowned.

'I can't believe anyone buys them to tell you the truth. Even I bought a new couch on the never-never. I'll have a black coffee if you've got one.'

'You can have anything you like. We've got a coffee machine. How about an espresso?'

'Too strong for me. An Americano would be nice. And a slice of that cake if you're offering.'

I wasn't, but I wanted to keep her relaxed so I could ask her some questions. I cut her a modest slice of lemon drizzle, but not so small she could complain. Her stroppy nature would not countenance a slight like that. I handed her the cake and she took a big bite, swallowing it almost without chewing. I wondered if she was hungry, but I didn't dare ask. She had that 'walking on eggshells' character, like a firework daring you to light it. I wondered if Lance had said something to upset her. I decided to add her to my list of suspects after she left.

'I heard they let your boy Cracker out of the nick,' I said, attempting familiarity. 'My stepson is a friend of his, you know.'

She looked at me suspiciously.

'What's his name?'

'Mouse.'

She cackled.

'Oh, I know him. Handsome lad. He helped Cracker unlock his phone.'

'Did he? That was nice of him.'

As long as the phone wasn't stolen… I crossed my fingers.

'The police couldn't hold my son any longer. He hadn't done nothing,' said Delia.

Nothing except mug Grace, but I guessed she hadn't pressed charges.

'Did you meet Lance before he died?'

She shook her head and a shadow passed over her face.

'When I heard he'd be coming to the Pavilion, I went over there to talk to the manager. Reg something.'

'Dolan.'

'Yes. I wanted to know when Lance was arriving and if I could meet him.'

'What did Reg say?'

She grinned at me, showing her blackened teeth.

'I thought he would have a heart attack when I walked in. He clasped his chest and fell backwards into his chair.

'What did he say?'

'Marge. He said it two or three times.'

'He thought you were Marge?'

'I guess so. People say I look just like her.'

'They're right. You're practically a clone. What happened with Reg?'

'After he calmed down a little, I told him Marge was my mother, is my mother. He kept staring at me, really creepy you know. And then he asked me why I wanted to see Lance.'

'What did you tell him?'

'That Lance was my father. He asked me if I was sure, and I said Marge told me a few years ago when I traced her.' A single tear coursed down her cheek. 'They took me away from her because he wouldn't marry her, you know.'

'Marge told me. I'm really sorry that happened to you. It must have been tough.'

'I didn't know I had been adopted until I found a certificate when my mother died, my adoptive mother. It made perfect sense once I knew. I never felt like part of that family. They treated me like shit and I started staying out late and getting into trouble in my teenage years. I still drink too much now, but I try to control it.'

'I can't imagine what you went through. Did you ask Reg about Marge?'

'Like what? I know they worked together years ago with Lance, but he didn't talk to me about it.'

I wondered if I should tell Delia about her mother and Reg, but it didn't seem like my place. The fact Delia had told Reg about Lance being her father rang alarm bells in my head. Reg had told me he looked forward to seeing Lance again, but Lance had ruined his life, and now he had proof in the form of Delia. Her visit must have shocked him to the core. Could mild-mannered Reg Dolan be a murderer? I found it hard to believe. There was one thing she could clear up though.

'I nearly forgot,' I said. 'My son Mouse left his Seagulls' scarf in the Shanty one night and Joy Wells told me she gave it to you. That scarf had sentimental value for him, so I wondered if you might consider giving it back to me. I can buy you a new scarf from the football club if you want one.'

Delia drew her eyebrows together and scratched her neck.

'The scarf? I'd be happy to give it back to Mouse, but I haven't seen it for ages. Come to think of it, I wore it to the Pavilion that day.'

'The day you went to see Reg?'

'Yes. It went with my outfit. I can't remember seeing it since. I must have left it on the bus, or dropped it when I walked home.'

'Could you have left it at the Pavilion?'

'I might have. I don't remember. What's so important about the scarf?'

'Nothing really. Just my stepson's obsession with it. Did Cracker give you Lance's ring?'

'What ring? I don't know nothing about no ring.'

I could have banged my head on the table, I felt so stupid.

'I guess the murderer stole it,' I said. 'Lance had a ring he claimed he got from Frank Sinatra, but no one believed him. Marge told me it was hers, an inheritance from her grandmother, and that Lance took it from her when they worked together.'

Delia snorted with laughter.

'Ain't no one gonna leave nothing to Marge. Her family disowned her for becoming a dancer on the stage. She probably got it from an admirer when she worked in the theatre. She told me it was like taking candy from babies in them days. But then she got pregnant and it ruined her career.'

'She must be resentful. I know I would be.'

'She should have hated Lance, I did, but she waited all these years hoping he'd come back to her. Love's a funny thing.'

'It sure is.'

Later that evening I discovered I had received a text from Cracker. I assumed Marge had given him my number. I had missed it because I had put my phone on silent to concentrate on the accounts. It read – *'I think I know who murdered Lance. No police. Can you meet me?'*.

A shiver of excitement ran up my back. I wondered what Delia had said to him about our chat. Had something triggered a memory? I tried to call him back, but he didn't answer. No doubt he had gone to the pub and couldn't hear it. Or perhaps he only liked to text. I knew Mouse was allergic to calls, like all young people his age. Cracker was only a few years older. I texted him back saying he could come by the Vintage any time for coffee and a chat. I couldn't wait to hear what he had to say. Maybe we finally got a breakthrough in the case.

Chapter 28

Whatever else I expected the police to find in the basement, another body had not figured on that list. George had called me in a state of high excitement, not long after I arrived at Second Home. According to him, the victim had been shoved into a flight case, one of the ubiquitous cases with silver corners found backstage in every theatre and film production. They were used to transport everything from make-up to lighting rigs. Their rectangular shape made them easy to store and ship. They were not made to hide bodies, or other vessels with fluids in. D.I. Antrim had been almost hysterical with fury when George told him about the murder. He had come to Seacastle to demonstrate his superiority as a detective, but had ended up with two unsolved murders instead of one. George had chuckled down the phone as he described the D.I. arriving on scene, but couldn't give me details as he got interrupted.

Harry and I had arrived early at the shop with the intention of polishing the tops of the lacquered tables I had salvaged from the Italian café. I know it doesn't sound romantic, but until Roz turned up unexpectedly, Harry and I had managed to get a lot of fun out of polishing the tables and snogging behind the wardrobes. Roz arrived pink-cheeked after cycling across town from Pirate's Harbour. She had been on her husband's fishing boat overnight and her twinkling eyes told tales about Ed's mood. The kelp sanctuary offshore had not been the disaster that many had predicted. Ed had found new clients for lobsters and crabs which he now fished more often. Lobsters fetched a premium price and he had found a secret area where they were more abundant.

I had hoped to be alone with Harry, because we still hadn't managed to talk about his brother or our patchy relationship. He had taken Roz's arrival with good humour and a gentle roll of his eyes. Harry liked Roz's unfiltered stream of consciousness which gave him an excuse not to speak. I couldn't tell her to go away and let us have a moment, because she loved to gossip and would only invent something annoying. The three of us had got into a rhythm with the cleaning and had almost finished by the time Flo turned up, huffing and puffing, her messy bun even wilder than usual. She wore a pink smock which made her look like a cupcake. She leaned against the counter, panting and getting her breath back while we all surrounded her waiting for whatever revelation had brought her to the Second Home at midday.

'You'll never believe it,' she said, wiping her brow. 'The police search of the basement at the Pavilion has uncovered a body.'

A collective gasp greeting this news. George had only told me about the body on pain of death if I revealed the secret, so I pretended to be shocked too. Flo nodded.

'It looks like the same murderer, but I can't be sure yet.'

'It's like an Agatha Christie mystery,' said Roz. 'I love those. But there is no butler to blame this time.'

'I think we are due a coffee break,' I said.

'I'll do the honours,' said Roz. 'Would you prefer a pot of Earl Grey, Flo.'

'Oh, yes, please. Give me a minute to crawl up the stairs.'

Harry gave her his arm and took the strain as she wilted about half way up. Roz had already cut a large moist slice of banana bread, and placed it in front of Flo who took a grateful bite. We waited for her to pour herself a cup of tea and sip it with caution before asking her any questions.

'Give us a blow-by-blow account,' said Roz, pulling her feet underneath her body on the banquette and covering her legs with her skirt.

'I can't tell you everything, and this information is confidential until it is announced, but one of the officers searching the scene for clues to Lance's murder, found a trickle of liquid. He followed it to one of the flight cases and opened it. Inside he made the gruesome discovery of a male body.'

'What's a flight case?' said Harry.

'One of those black cases with silver edges they use for storing things backstage,' I said. 'Who is it?'

'I can't confirm yet,' said Flo. 'It's a man.'

'Hunter Norman?' I said. 'But who would kill him?'

'I didn't say it was him. You're not at liberty to tell anybody yet. Not until I confirm the identity.'

'How did he die?' said Harry.

'Ah, I'm on my way to the lab to find out. They've brought the whole flight case in, so I can examine it for clues.'

'That's some turn up for the books,' said Harry. 'I wonder who it is.'

'They won't let us into the theatre to find out, that's for sure,' I said.

'I've got to go now. D.I. Antrim will have a kitten if I keep him waiting. I'll let you know who it is, and how he died, when I do.'

'I have a feeling it will be Hunter,' I said. 'Olivia saw him hanging around in the basement just before Lance's body was discovered. And Hunter claimed to be Lance's son.'

'His son?' said Flo. 'Didn't he ever use a condom?'

'I can imagine lots of reasons why someone murdered Lance,' I said. 'But Hunter seemed so vanilla. Just another wannabe star getting too old for his lucky break. I even considered he might have killed Lance to get his chance in the spotlight.'

'This Lance sounds like catnip for women,' said Roz. 'A bit like David Foster, and look what happened to him.'

'I wouldn't discount professional jealousy,' said Harry. 'If as you told me Lance had hogged the spotlight for years, the whole cast had reasons to want him gone.'

'If they murdered Hunter, that would still make sense,' I said. 'He told me he would be next to dominate after Lance retired.'

Flo did not comment. For once her lips were sealed. I wondered if it was really Hunter in that flight case. I'd have to wait to find out.

After Flo had left, we were deflated by the lack of information. If Hunter had been murdered, most of my theories were incorrect. Why would Delia or Reg kill Hunter? Or Cracker? I would have to review everyone's motives and start again. The thought that Olivia had a motive crept into my head, but I pushed it out again. Olivia could not kill anyone. She would get someone else to do it. Roz stood up.

'I've got to go,' she said. 'I promised Ed I'd go to the supermarket. Our food supplies are mirroring the Antarctic, a few Penguins and some frozen fish.'

'I could make a delicious meal from that,' said Harry.

'No, you couldn't,' I said, punching his arm.

Roz skipped down the stairs.

'Thanks for tolerating the gooseberry in your midst,' she said. 'I promise I'll keep quiet until Flo gives us the official version.'

'I thought you said gorilla in the mist,' I said. 'I must be going deaf.'

'That's my fault. You know what makes you deaf,' said Harry, and he winked. 'I'm sorry I haven't been around much.'

'I'm a policeman's ex-wife. I had to carry a photo of George in my wallet so I could remember what he looked like.'

'I'm not sure I'd forget that face.'

'Don't be mean. George is doing his best. Sharon is being mean to him again. I don't hold out much hope of their relationship surviving.'

'But I don't want you thinking I don't care about you.'

'If finding your brother is important to you, it's important to me too. Have you made any progress?'

'I saw him.'

'You did? What happened?'

'He didn't see me though.'

'Oh, you were spying on him?'

'I wouldn't call it spying. I just wanted to make sure he looked okay. You know, healthy.'

'And did he?'

'Thin, he looked very thin, and tired and I wanted to talk to him, but I couldn't.'

'But why? You'd driven all that way.'

Harry's head sunk into his hands.

'Fear. He doesn't want to be found. I thought I might ruin his peace. He lives in the middle of nowhere in an old cottage. Maybe, he'd be better off if he never saw me again.'

I kissed his bald head and put my arm around his muscular shoulders.

'Do you want to tell me what happened to drive you apart?'

'I'm ashamed, and afraid you'll think less of me.'

'You need to trust me, partner. We're in the same troop now, remember you told me that? Whatever it is, I'll stand by you.'

'It happened after Cathy died, when I was drinking far too much. I know that's not an excuse, but I had broken inside, and I struggled to regain control for ages.'

'You told me about the drinking.'

'Well, Nick sent his girlfriend to see me, to make sure I could cope. What he didn't know is that she had a massive crush on me. I always avoided being in the same room as her without somebody else present.'

'She wouldn't take no for an answer?'

'I literally had to fight her off. I might have been drunk, but I still had morals. Unfortunately, she took rejection badly. She went straight home to my brother and claimed I had tried to take her by force.'

'That's terrible.'

'She showed him bruises and claimed I had hit her, but I swear I didn't touch her. I think she may have inflicted them herself. Nick rang me up and told me he never wanted to see me again. He wouldn't listen to me when I swore I hadn't touched her. That's when I stopped drinking, because I needed to be sure nobody could ever take advantage of me again. I think it's why I can't...'

'I'm so sorry. No wonder you're struggling. I don't mind at all, you know. We're not in a hurry. When you're ready, tell me. I'm not going anywhere.'

'But George—'

'I don't love George anymore. I love you. Will you tell me about the army?'

'Another day. It's hard for me to tell you about my failures. I want to be a knight in shining armour for you, not the weedy candle-lighter in the local church.'

'I happen to like candle lighters. Come on baby, light my fire comes to mind.'

'Hilarious. Tell me about the case. It sounds like a doozy.'

'Did I tell you someone hired me to find out the truth?'

'No, but you're about to.'

Chapter 29

Cracker never called me back. He didn't get the chance because someone had doped him with Rohypnol and strangled him with a scarf from the theatre's extensive wardrobe. George called me to let me know, which of course he shouldn't have. He swore me to secrecy and I walked around like a zombie until Flo gave me the all clear. I felt profoundly depressed by Cracker's demise. Ghita burst into tears when I told her, and Mouse became withdrawn and sad. I couldn't bear to imagine the pain poor Delia and Marge were experiencing. It seemed like a bad dream. I asked Flo about Lance's ring, but it had gone missing again. I couldn't help feeling that the murders were not unrelated to it. After all, if it was really Frank Sinatra's, it would be worth a lot of money.

The police had no leads, other than the marked similarity to the first murder. The forensic team took DNA samples from everyone in the cast of the show, and all the people who worked in the theatre, and sent them for analysis. I wondered how the forensic team would react when Lance turned out to have at least two children in the suspect list. It occurred to me that maybe Cynthia had gathered Lance's offspring in Seacastle for a final showdown, but the idea struck me as so ludicrous I dismissed it again. I needed to speak to Reg. He had not told me about speaking to Delia. I sent him a text asking him if he would meet me in the Ocean Café, but he didn't reply. Cynthia didn't answer either. I felt deflated as it became more obvious that I had been shut out.

It didn't take the Superintendent long to become disillusioned with D.I. Antrim's handling of the Lance Emerald case. He had only been given it in the first place because of Mouse and me being suspects. The Super couldn't point to any noticeable improvement in the progress of the investigation with D.I. Antrim involved, and I suspected Flo of sabotage in the slowness of her forensic examinations. When D.I. Antrim had been sent back to Brighton, I received a call from George who sounded cock-a-hoop.

'Guess what, Tan? I've been reassigned to the case, well, both cases as it happens.'

I waited for him to thank me for all my help, but I should have known it wouldn't be forthcoming. I forced myself to congratulate him.

'Well done. That's great news. You must be thrilled,' I said, through gritted teeth.

'Sharon's taking me out to dinner,' he said.

'Great. I'm glad you two sorted it out.'

'Um, look, I don't want you interfering with the case anymore.'

What a cheek! My head almost exploded with fury. Almost everything he knew about the case, I had told him, but now he wanted to go it alone again.

'Interfering? Is that what I was doing?' I said.

For once he picked up on my change of tone.

'There's no need to get all snotty on me. You're not a member of the police force. It isn't protocol to have you involved.'

'Protocol? I've a good mind to tell Sharon about you sneaking over to eat in my house when she doesn't feed you properly.'

He spluttered.

'Don't do that. She'd skin me alive.'

'You're not welcome at the Grotty Hovel anymore. Stay away, or I'll tell her all about you; and I mean all.'

'You don't really mean that. And don't call my house the Grotty Hovel. I paid good money for it.'

'Your house? I believe it's in my name. And yes, I do mean it. And I have a job to do too, interviewing the main suspects. I'm being paid and I intend to honour my contract.'

'Contract? Who'd hire you? You're not a private detective.'

'I am now. Goodbye George.'

But I wasn't convinced I could face it any more. In a strange way, I felt as if it was my fault Cracker had been murdered. I had missed something vital, maybe even obvious, and now someone had killed him. I couldn't imagine why. Of course, they might have killed him out of a desire for revenge. Many people still thought they knew who killed Lance, and Cracker remained the prime suspect. Both men had been killed by drugging them with Rohypnol and strangling them, but that didn't mean there weren't two different murderers. Copycat murders were common on the TV, but I didn't know how often they happened in real life. In fact, I didn't know much of anything.

My confidence collapsed and I stayed away from the Pavilion sulking in the shop. I amused myself by hanging out with Ghita and the boys over at Surfusion. They had made progress on putting in the kitchen and were planning elaborate testing menus. The Tribute competition had been postponed for two weeks, so at Reg's request, Mouse returned to the Pavilion to help an increasingly hysterical Reg to reissue the tickets and fill the empty seats. Personally, I couldn't believe people still wanted to come to the scene of two recent murders, or perhaps that's why they were coming? I couldn't decide. Helen and Olivia had taken themselves along the coast to Brighton for shopping, and tours of the Brighton Pavilion.

'Swapping one pavilion for another,' said Helen, with forced gaiety.

Harry called me just when I got to the end of my tether.

'Hello there, partner. Fancy coming on a clearance with me tomorrow?'

'Do you need to ask?'

'Great. See you at dawn.'

'Dawn?'

'Eight o'clock.'

'That's my kind of dawn.'

'Please can you make some bacon butties and a flask of tea for breakfast?'

'Of course.'

I wandered over to Surfusion to see if Ghita had time for a chat, but she had gone to Brighton with Rohan and Kieron. I pulled my jacket tighter around me as a chill autumn breeze whipped up the high street. I contemplated walking down to Grace's shop for a gossip, but then I remembered she and Max had one of their big buyers in for a private viewing. I headed for the Ocean Café, meaning to have a solitary coffee and a sulk. That would mean passing by the Pavilion Theatre, but I couldn't avoid it for ever. Final rehearsals were on, meaning that everyone would be there and as I neared it, the temptation to pop in and have a nose around became irresistible.

I hovered at the back of the theatre, debating the wisdom of entering, when I saw Marge and Delia walking along the pier arm in arm. My heart broke for them. What a bitter blow for Delia after finally reuniting her family, to see it blown apart by a double murder. Unsure of my welcome, I followed them towards the café, catching up as they reached the entrance.

'It's you,' said Delia. 'Mouse's mother.'

'That's right.'

'She's also a private detective,' said Marge. 'She's famous.'

I shook my head.

'I'm a fraud. Cracker and Lance are dead, and I couldn't stop the murderer. I'm so sorry for your loss. I don't know what to say.'

Delia sniffed. Her features were drawn and her hair ratty. Her baggy tracksuit had several large stains and a couple of cigarette burns on it. She looked exactly what she was, a mother who had lost a son. I pushed the door open for them and followed them in. We went up to the mezzanine lounge and sat in the window overlooking the sea. I hadn't intended to sit with them. It just happened. I tried to imagine how I could offer them any condolences adequate for the enormity of the loss they had suffered. Strangely, they seemed more worried about me.

'Now, dear. You're not to blame yourself. Lance got what he deserved. You can't go through your whole life treating people like that and hope they'll forgive and forget. You don't imagine we're his only victims, do you?'

'The police don't have a hope of finding the killer. There are so many suspects,' said Delia. 'I would have killed him myself if I got the chance. But I didn't. Whoever used the scarf to strangle Lance intended to frame me.'

'Are you sure Cracker didn't take it?'

'Are you saying my lad killed Lance? They've killed him too,' said Delia, whose hard exterior crumbled as she wept into a dirty napkin someone had left on the table.

'I'm so sorry. That's not what I meant at all. We all believed Cracker was innocent. My son is heartbroken.'

'He was never going to make old bones,' said Marge. 'But he didn't deserve to die.'

'I loved him. He was my little boy. Someone took him away from me. And I need them to pay for it,' said Delia.

'The police are working on it,' I said. 'My ex-husband is in charge of the case now. He's a good policeman.'

'I don't trust the police,' said Marge. 'I want you to carry on. There's even more reason now.'

'But where would I start?'

'With the cast. They'll all be using stage names. Many of them have something to hide. You need to follow their trails and find out where they came from. Lance spread his seed far and wide. Maybe I'm not the only one with a grievance.'

'Perhaps you should be the detective rather than me. You seem to have it all figured out,' I said.

'You're the one with the skills. I'm too old to go running around and using computers.'

'You have the perfect cover,' said Delia. 'Who's going to be suspicious of a journalist asking questions? It's your job.'

'But I failed completely to stop them. I don't know if I'm up to it.'

'You couldn't have known they would come for Cracker too. I've been blaming myself for telling him about Lance, and that accursed ring. He only went there for the ring you know. He had no interest in his grandfather.'

I found her harsh take a little shocking, but I felt cheered by their support. Mouse could carry out some wizardry on the computer and give me leads George would never come up with. The only way to get to the bottom of this was to go back to the beginning of the saga and work our way forward. I sighed.

'Okay. But I need you to tell me the whole truth about Lance and Reg and Cynthia first. I can't figure this out if I don't know what happened then.'

Marge sighed.

'I'll tell you. But I need a drink first.'

'Let's finish these coffees and go to the Shanty.'

Chapter 30

Joy Wells raised an eyebrow when I arrived at the Shanty with Marge and Delia in tow. She gave us the snug in the corner so we could have some privacy, not that we needed any at that time in the evening. The sun had only just begun to exit stage right when we entered through the tiny door into the comforting embrace of the cosy pub. A couple of regulars from the fishing fraternity were exchanging yarns and tucking into a steak and kidney pie, but we were essentially alone. I ordered the drinks and waited for Marge to pluck up the courage to tell me the truth about Lance Emerald.

It turned out that Marge needed more than one drink to unlock the secrets she had hidden so long. I tempered my impatience when I realised Delia had not heard this version of events either. It would be hard for her to hear what had transpired, and Marge might be ashamed to tell her. Marge had lied to herself and everyone else so long that she struggled to untangle what was true from what was made up. She made several false starts and meandered off into anecdotes about some young man who fancied her in Blackpool or Brighton. I hoped I had enough in my bank balance to extract all the information I needed. I signalled Joy to keep them coming.

By the time Marge felt able to tell me the truth, she was already three sheets to the wind. Delia had joined her in downing a couple of stiff vodka and tonics and she sat back, looking droopy and absent. I leaned forward and prodded Marge into life again. She grumbled and frowned and played with the ice in her drink. Just when I began to doubt I would ever get anything out of her, she perked up and started to speak.

'We were all so close in them days,' she said. 'Me and Thia were like peas in a pod. We shared our clothes and makeup, and jewels and admirers. What a pair we were! Nobody was safe when Marge and Thia were in town.'

'I'll bet you rang rings around them,' I said. 'What about Reg and Lance?'

'Oh, them too. Thia had a thing for Lance, and he had a thing for me. But Reg had already laid claim to these territories, so Lance stayed away. Thia thought Lance loved her, but I knew, yes, I did. Lance loved me most. They were often out on the town with punters. We all were. They were generous and fun. We didn't make much money, so we let people take us out and buy champagne and presents. But afterwards, Reg would come home with me and Thia would go home with Lance.'

Marge stopped talking and her eyes had a faraway look in them, as if she could see a film of the past running in her mind.

'So why did you leave the group?' I said.

'Leave where?' she said, looking around, as if surprised to find herself in the Shanty. 'My drink's empty.'

She shook her glass in my face, the cubes of ice clinking against the sides. A drop of condensation fell onto her pink skirt and made a dark stain like blood spreading on a pavement. I caught Joy's eye and she brought over a refill. I whispered in her ear to make a pot of coffee, but I had my doubts we would get Marge back along the cliffs to the carpark. The Shanty had a glorious view, but nobody claimed it was easy to get to, or from.

Her glass replenished, Marge sighed.

'One time we were playing at the Palace Theatre in Southend-on-Sea. Reg and Thia both had the flu and were confined to bed for a few days. They had to be isolated so they didn't pass it on to us. Lance and I found ourselves thrown together, as it were.'

She smirked at the thought and took a swig of her drink. I prayed she'd get through her tale before I had to buy another.

'They didn't know, Reg and Thia. About us, I mean. We had a couple of nights together. I've never been so happy. Lance told me he had had an offer to go solo, but he wanted to finish the season to be fair to Reg. I just wanted to be with Lance.'

'But then Reg and Thia got better?'

'That were hard. I couldn't stand for Reg to touch me anymore, but I had to pretend. Lance didn't skip a beat. He went straight back to Thia as if nothing had happened.'

'But something had?'

'I missed my period. I couldn't believe it. We were always so careful in them days. Getting pregnant spelled the end of everything. I would have to get married or my life would be ruined. No more dancing, no more parties. But when I told Lance he said he wouldn't marry me. He asked me how I knew it wasn't Reg's. And the awful truth is that I didn't know. I thought I did, but I couldn't prove it. I couldn't tell Reg it was his, in case it came out looking like Lance. So I ran away and stayed with an aunt of mine who took pity on me. At least I thought she did.'

She stopped and gazed out of the window.

'But she gave your baby away,' I said. 'And told you she had died.'

Marge sniffed.

'How was I to know? I was only a baby myself. I grieved for the baby and then I went on with my life. But I couldn't help waiting for Lance. No one came close to him. I just couldn't find anyone else.'

'And then I found you,' said Delia, who had been mute until then.

Marge beamed.

'Yes, you did, angel. Easily the best day of my life. When you came through the door, it were like looking at me in a time travel mirror.'

'You could be twins,' I said. 'It's uncanny. No wonder Reg nearly had a heart attack when you walked into his office.'

Marge's brow furrowed and she drew her brows together.

'Could it be Reg what done it?' she said.

'The murders?' I said.

'Yes, both of them. Maybe when he found out what Lance did and why I ran away?'

The idea had occurred to me too. I had dismissed it as unlikely. But now Cracker had been murdered too, I had to admit the possibility.

'What about Cynthia, Thia? Is she capable of murder? What if they ganged up on you?'

'I hadn't thought of that. They say revenge is a dish best eaten cold, but why would she wait all this time?'

'Maybe she didn't know until now either,' said Delia. 'She could have found my scarf, if I dropped it.'

'Or you might have left it in Reg's office,' I said.

'I can't bear to think about it,' said Marge.

'I promise to do everything I can to find out the truth,' I said. 'But I have one more question for you.'

'Last one. My mother's tired,' said Delia, patting Marge's hand.

'Why did Lance run away to France, if nobody knew he was the father of Marge's baby?'

'Oh, that was later,' said Marge. 'He had a solo act for several years in the West End. He almost made big time.'

'Is that when Frank Sinatra gave him the ring?' I said.

Marge pursed her lips.

'Why are you still on about that? I told you it was my grandmother's. I should get it back. He stole it.'

She started to weep and staggered off to the toilet. Delia shook her head at me.

'That's enough. Can't you see you're upsetting her?'

'Whoever killed Cracker stole the ring from him. If it was really Frank Sinatra's, it is worth a great deal of money. That's a big motive for murder. The person who killed Cracker may have used a scarf to make it look like the same person murdered him as Lance. There could be two killers. I want to be very sure about the ring, and I'm not convinced Marge is telling the truth. I'm sorry.'

'I'll find out for you. Just leave her alone. She's done her time.'

'One last thing. Do you know what Lance Emerald's real name was?'

She smiled.

'Marge told me it was Jimmy Dymond, get it?'

I got it.

When Marge came back from the toilet, her breath smelled of vomit, but she seemed much chirpier. Joy poured us some coffee, and we ate some crisps to fortify us for the walk along the cliffs. I rang the local taxi and asked him to ferry us home from the car park. Then we staggered along the path with Marge singing snatches of old music hall hits and Delia smoking roll ups. I nearly begged for a puff, but I felt as if I'd got myself in enough trouble for one night.

Chapter 31

The next morning, a wave of nausea came over me as I fried the bacon for the butties requested by Harry. I had almost forgotten we had a clearance until his text message reminding me woke me up. I threw on my clothes and washed my teeth twice, but I couldn't rid myself of the taste of hangover. Mouse stomped down the stairs when the smell of bacon crept under his door and penetrated his sleep. I had added extra slices to the grill to forestall his whinging, if he didn't get a butty too. He screwed his eyes up as he examined me.

'I heard you come in late last night. Don't you think you're burning the candle at both ends?'

'I met Marge and Delia on the pier yesterday and our coffee together turned into a session in the Shanty.'

'They must be shattered. First Lance and then Cracker. It's horrible for them.'

'They want me to keep working on the case.'

'What case? Did you become a private detective without telling me?'

'Not exactly. It's a long story. Anyway, I've got lots of new information to help me get to the bottom of it. Are you game?'

He tightened the cord of his dressing gown and sat at the table buttering the bread for the butties.

'Do you have to ask? What can I do?'

'Lance set out on a solo career after he left the Balentine Brothers. He worked the clubs in London for a few years, but then he fled to France. Nobody knows why. I suspect, as Cindy said to me the other day, it's another case of cherchez la femme. Can you see if you can find anything on the internet about it? I reckon he worked in London most of the 90s.'

'Sure. I'll do it today. Do you know any details that might help me?'

'I know he worked at the 100 Club for a while. And his real name is Jimmy Dymond, so that should help.'

'I'll get right on it. Do you want me to open the café?'

'Yes, please. Roz will be in the shop today as well, so you can catch up on the gossip with her. Find out if she has come up with anything relating to Lance or Marge. They're both from around here, so there might be information you can follow up.'

'Okay. Where are you going today?'

'I don't know. We might deliver stuff to the East End, so let me know if you find anything I can research while I'm up in London.'

'Will do. Have a great day. I'm going back to bed.'

He wrapped his butty in paper towel and kissed the top of my head. I finished making the other butties and poured tea into a flask. I put them all in my satchel, and threw on a jacket and scarf. Hades got a piece of bacon too, as I ran an equal opportunity household. He grabbed it from me with glee and took it to his laundry basket to eat.

Harry drew up in the van as I stepped through the front door. He flashed the headlights at me and I scampered around to the passenger door. A smell of bacon infused the cabin making us both salivate with anticipation.

'I can't wait,' said Harry. 'Let's eat them on the sea front and drive on from there.'

'My wind shelter is closest, and we can give the crusts to Herbert.'

'You can give your crusts to him if you like. I'm starving. I'm not giving my breakfast to a seagull.'

'But he's so cute.'

'Only you would consider that hooligan as cute. He'll be stealing people's chips out of their hands soon.'

We parked opposite the wind shelter and dashed across the road. I handed Harry his sandwich and he bit into it with an expression of bliss. Is there anything as delicious as a butty with crispy bacon and ketchup sandwiched between two slices of fresh bread? I let the delicious smell and taste drown out my hangover. When I had finished, I placed my crusts on the bench between us while I poured us a cup of tea. Herbert arrived in a great flurry of wings and marched up and down in front of the shelter. I reached for the crusts to find Harry had picked them up and intended to eat them.

'I wouldn't do that if I were you,' I said. 'Herbert has a razor-sharp beak, and he's not afraid to use it.'

Harry chucked the crusts to Herbert with bad grace. I passed him a cup of tea, trying not to laugh at his sulky expression.

'Second in line to a seagull,' he said. 'I'll never live this down.'

Soon we were on the road again.

'Where are we going today?' I said.

'A cottage in Shoreham. The owners are moving to assisted living and they can't take everything with them.'

'It's always sad to clear a house, but these make me sadder.'

'At least they took their favourite pieces with them.'

'Life's weird that way.'

'How do mean?'

'We spend our youths longing for things we can't buy. Then, pass our adulthoods accumulating the things we can. And finally, we spend our old ages downsizing and getting rid of things.'

'Because you can't take it with you?'

'Exactly. That's why I'm sure Lance gave his ring to Cracker. He had terminal cancer. He knew he would be dead soon, so he gave his most treasured possession to his grandson.'

'We all seem to be assuming Lance is his grandfather. But are you sure? Have the DNA tests come back yet?

'I don't know. I need to ask Flo. But you're right. If Delia wasn't Lance's daughter, that changes everything, included possible motives. The result of the DNA tests could be the key to the murders.'

'Thank me later.'

He gave me a smug grin. Maggot. But he had hit the nail on the head. George always told me they investigated family members first when someone was murdered. But what if nobody knew who Lance's family were? We would have to start from the beginning again.'

'We're here,' Harry said, dragging me back to reality.

A scruffy cottage, set back from the road, sat in an overgrown garden. It had an exuberant covering of ivy which resembled a rock star afro. A dead log in the garden emphasised the image by resembling a large spliff. As we approached the house, a young man in a cheap suit came up the path in shoes with segs on the heels. The noise of the metal hitting the paving stones took me right back to the playground at school with the boys running around and dragging their shoes on the concrete. His hair had been cut short, and his face shone red with the closeness of his shave.

'Are you here to do the clearance?' he said.

'That's right,' said Harry.

'I've left the front door open. Can you tear up the carpets too?'

'I'm afraid we don't take carpets.'

'You can have everything in the house for free, if you take the carpets out.'

Harry rubbed his chin and looked at me. I shrugged.

'Have we got the tools?' I said.

'We have. Okay, we'll do it.'

He beamed.

'That's fantastic. Just leave the key under the plant pot by the front door.'

He marched past us, sparks flying, and jumped into a GTI Golf parked outside.

'Let's go and have a look,' I said.

'I hope it's worth it,' said Harry. 'It would have been more sensible to look first.'

We needn't have worried. A strong smell of patchouli hit us as we entered the remnants of a hippie palace. Indian shawls decorated the walls and hung over the archways. Old, red paper lampshades hang from the ceilings and red stained carpets covered the floors. Empty bookshelves still had the imprints in dust of the books which had been removed.

'We could be in the sixties,' I said.

'It looks rather dated now, doesn't it?'

I spotted a pair of lava lamps in the sitting room on the shelf over the fireplace. Bronze incense holders full of ash sat on several surfaces surrounded by overgrown plants and fallen leaves. A charming, Victorian pair of lovers' chairs sat alone in the room beside a square, blond-ash, coffee table. I squeaked with joy as I recognised the Ercol Pandora's box model. I could sell that in a minute at several hundred pounds. I pointed gleefully at it.

'The coffee table?' said Harry. 'Seriously?'

'It doesn't look like much, but it's a classic. I can sell that, or pass it on to Grace. The love seats are nice too.'

'Shall we try them?'

We sat back-to-back and Harry leaned over and kissed me. I sighed with bliss and kissed him back. We stayed there for ages kissing and giggling. Then, I felt something crawling up my leg. I jumped up and pulled up my trouser.

'Steady,' said Harry. 'Don't go getting all excited. Keep your clothes on.'

But then his brow creased and he reached down to scratch his leg.

'What the f—'

'Outside, quick,' I said. 'The place is crawling with fleas.'

We dashed outside and wiggled and jiggled and checked each other's clothes and found three fat fleas trying to hide in the seams. I am not squeamish, but fleas are revolting. I shuddered with revulsion. Harry laughed.

'No wonder he wanted us to take out the carpets. We'll have to buy some insecticide and some deet to spray on ourselves before we can do it. Take a quick whiz around the house to choose the furniture you want and, meanwhile, I'll nip into town and buy the supplies.'

'Can you get me a t-shirt and jeans from the charity shop please? I'll need to put these clothes into a sealed bag and straight into a boil wash before I wear them again.'

'Good plan. Back soon. Have fun with our friends.'

He drove off leaving me suffering an attack of the heebie-jeebies. Finally, I persuaded myself back into the house and did a high-speed recce. I grabbed the lava lamps and the lovers' seat, but I couldn't lift the coffee table. In the other room, I found a set of etched glass tumblers and a matching bottle in a soft blue colour with dolphin designs. Also, a beautiful Afghan rug, but I couldn't face the ordeal of trying to clean it. Hades would be impossible to treat if he got fleas. He had even tried to bite Mouse when he had treated him with his quarterly drops. Poor Mouse had not taken it well and they didn't snuggle for a couple of days after that.

On further searching, I found a 1950s' tall, lemon-yellow kitchen cabinet with glass doors on top, and a matching unit with two drawers and shelves below, neither of which I could take out without Harry. Then I felt a flea creeping along the line of my bra. I ran back outside into a large shrub and took my top off. I looked around, and seeing no one about, took off my bra and started to whip it around my head. The cool wind felt rather nice and I stood for a minute whirling my bra around, while I enjoyed the unusual sensation. Suddenly, someone coughed nearby. I covered by breasts with my hands, mortified.

'Is that some sort of female religious ritual? Or can we all join in?'

The young man had returned. My cheeks blazed with embarrassment.

'Turn around and don't look,' I said, although I suspected he had already had an eyeful.

I shook my shirt out vigorously and put it back on, hanging my bra on a branch and leaving it there. I emerged from the bush to find him smirking.

'If you'd told us about the fleas, I wouldn't be stripping off in the garden,' I said. 'This is one hundred percent your fault.'

'I should have told you. Where's your colleague?' he said, leering at me.

'He'll be back in a minute,' I said, looking around.

'How long's a minute?'

I realised with shock that he might be considering assaulting me.

'What do you want?' I said, as aggressively as I could, while I tried to get nearer to the pavement.

'I'd have thought that was obvious,' he said, stroking his chin.

Luckily, Harry arrived at that moment and his antenna did not fail him. He was at my side before I drew another breath.

'Are you all right darling?' he said.

'Yes, Mr, um?'

'Colthard. I wanted to tell you to burn the carpets.'

'Is that because of the fleas?' I said.

'Oh, you noticed,' he said.

'Noticed?' said Harry. 'We were almost eaten alive.'

'Well, yes, I, er, must be going.'

He took off almost at a run. Harry had puffed out his chest, and not many men thought they could take him on once they notice his posture.

'Did he hurt you?'

'Only my pride. He saw me dancing nude in that shrub, the one with the bra hanging from its foliage.'

Harry laughed.

'No wonder he looked flushed. I'll spray the carpets, and we can come back in an hour or two when the fleas are dead. How about I treat you to a curry and a pint?'

'That sounds great. Did you buy me a clean shirt?'

Chapter 32

We had the most delicious curry for lunch and by the time we got back to the cottage, we felt fortified for the task of removing the furniture and the carpets. I changed back into my original clothes in case any of the original inhabitants of the carpets had survived the chemical onslaught. First, we carried out the pieces we were going to keep. Almost everything left in the cottage had some value so we took it all. I had snaffled the best bits for my shop, and Harry would take the rest to London with the other furniture he had already collected. His cousin Tommy had a warehouse in the East End, which we had visited a couple of times to deliver stuff I couldn't sell in the shop.

Once the house had been emptied, Harry took his claw hammer and a pair of pliers out of his tool box and we went back into the house. Harry opened the back door to let the breeze blow through the house from back to front and get rid of the worst of the chemical odour. We tied plastic bags around our knees to avoid the insecticide and made our way around the edge of the carpet pulling out the nails. The smell got right up my nose, and my eyes watered, but I resisted the temptation to rub them. I tried to concentrate on the task and not on the thought of all those dead bodies in the carpet.

We finished quickly and then rolled up the carpets and dragged them outside. Harry spilled a little gasoline from his spare tank on top of the revolting pile and I chucked a match on them. They caught fire immediately and crackled and hissed as the fire spread through the various bundles. I could almost see the bodies of the fleas exploding. While they burned, we checked the inside of the house again. The Indian hangings still hung on the walls, but we left them there, uncertain of their flea content. I picked up an incense holder from the windowsill in the shape of Ganesha, the elephant headed Hindu god of beginnings. Ghita had told me that people called him the remover of obstacles, who they invoked before starting a new venture to ease the difficulties that could arise. Ghita and the boys would need all the help they could get with their new restaurant, and I wasn't fussy where I found it. The handsome piece could sit above their doorway and lure the punters with his trunk.

As I was leaving the house, I noticed a loose floorboard. All the other boards were nailed down tightly so it looked out of place. Despite my whole body telling me to get out of the house, I couldn't resist lifting the plank using Harry's claw hammer. I peered into the space under the board and saw a plastic bag which I took out between the tips of my thumb and forefinger. Inside the bag, I saw some green organic material. I took a sniff and smiled at Harry.

'Two naughty old people,' I said. 'I bet their son had no idea what they smoked at home.'

'Do you want it?'

'Nope. Makes me vomit. I tried a few times with the same result.'

'Me either. Let's chuck it on the fire.'

Soon the sweet smell of marijuana seeped out of the fire's still hot embers. I felt sad for the old couple without their stash in assisted living. They'd have to subsist on lemon drizzle instead. More calories and less giggling.

We shut the door of the house and headed back to the van. I had put on the shirt and cargo trousers Harry had bought in the charity shop. The trousers were too loose and the shirt too tight. I had put my bra back on after reviewing it for fleas, but the gapping in the blouse made it a bit pointless. Harry couldn't help glancing over and grinning as he drove back to Seacastle.

'Keep your eyes on the road, soldier,' I said, but he ignored me.

Mouse waited for us at the shop and we carried in the new stock after spraying it with insecticide to be sure it didn't have any passengers.

'Honestly, you two. How does it take all day to collect a few sticks of furniture and a couple of lamps? And why don't you read your messages? I've been trying to contact you all day.'

I took my phone out of my handbag and, sure enough, there were five missed messages from Mouse.

'Sorry, sweetheart. We had an infestation of fleas to deal with which meant we had to stop for an enormous curry.'

'Neither of those explain why you didn't check your phone. Have you got it on silent again?'

'Of course not. I, oh…'

It's not my fault. I often put it on silent when I'm busy. I didn't see why I have to be at its beck and call all day. We missed lots of calls before mobile phones and no one died. Or perhaps they did, but we never found out. Anyway, I had, at least, started to take it with me everywhere which counted as a win, even if I forgot to take it off silent. I shrugged.

'It's on now. Why did you try and contact me? Did you find out anything about Lance?'

Mouse rolled his eyes.

'I did, as a matter of fact, and it could be important.'

'Isn't it tea time?' said Harry. 'I could devour a piece of Ghita's cake of the week. What flavour is it?'

'Plum and raisin cake,' said Mouse. 'It's a fruit cake, but it's delicious.'

'What have you got against fruit cakes?' I said.

'You didn't taste my mother's attempts,' said Mouse. 'She tried, but she wasn't much of a cook.'

'My Cathy couldn't boil an egg when I met her,' said Harry. 'I had to teach her how to cook. And I'm not Raymond Blanc.'

'At least Tanya's got that down to a T.'

They both chortled. I noticed they had both got to the stage where they could talk about their departed loved one with humour as well as sorrow.

'Very funny. I'll make a pot of tea if you cut the cake, Mouse. And don't cut huge slices. We're eating all the profits.'

Soon we were settled on the banquettes munching Ghita's cake. Even Mouse made some appreciative sounds. The cake slices disappeared and only crumbs remained as evidence of their passing. Harry burped loudly and I tutted at him.

'Quick, Mouse. Tell us about your findings before she blows a gasket,' he said.

Mouse brushed the crumbs from his t-shirt and took out his phone.

'Where do I start? Okay, Lance got a gig in London in May 1992 in the 100 Club in Oxford Street. That's the same month Frank Sinatra performed at the Albert Hall. So, the story about the ring could be true. After the 100 Club, he performed in various high end London clubs and even got a write up in the Evening Standard.'

'Always flirting with fame. That's our Lance,' said Harry.

'Always flirting full stop,' I said. 'The man was insatiable.'

'Anyway,' said Mouse. 'Not long after this article, there's a mention of the police looking for a certain Jimmy Dymond. Apparently, our man absconded to France, but it doesn't say why, or mention that Lance and Jimmy are the same person.'

'We need to find out why Lance left the country. How do we locate someone who might have information about the seedier side of London at the time,' I said.

'I'm pretty sure my cousin Tommy can help us,' said Harry. 'He knows some of the former club bouncers from the West End clubs, and a few retired coppers too. I'll give him a ring and see if he can do some research for us.'

'I'll come up to London with you when you deliver the furniture to him. Maybe we can question anyone he comes up with.'

'I have to ask him first.'

'Tanya is not famous for her patience,' said Mouse.

'So how come I put up with you two?'

'Fair point,' said Harry.

Chapter 33

I couldn't wait to get to Second Home the next morning. I almost ran along the promenade with hardly a glance at the shimmering sea or the wind farm. The lure of new stock always had the same effect on me as presents under the Christmas tree. Even though I knew what I had, the anticipation of touching them, cleaning them, and distributing them around the shop couldn't be beaten. I strode up King Street and juddered to a halt at the corner. George stood outside my shop shielding his eyes and trying to look in through the glass. I signed inwardly at the thought of having to deal with him instead of playing with my treasures. I plastered a faked smile on my face.

'To what do I owe this pleasure?' I said.

'Oh, hi Tan. Any chance of a coffee?' he said.

I wondered how he'd take it if I refused, but I had more than enough drama in my life without George having a tantrum. He might have some updates on the case too. I stuck the key in the lock and opened the door, showing him in. He headed straight upstairs, but instead of sitting down he stared longingly at the cake cabinet where the remains of Ghita's raisin and plumb cake sat moist on the plate. I rolled my eyes.

'I'm guessing you're still on a diet?'

'It's getting worse. I can't think about anything except food. She keeps forcing me to eat fruit instead of toast.'

'Why don't you have a piece of fruit cake? Then you can tell her you stuck to your diet. I'll make some coffee.'

By the time I turned around again, he was stuffing the last morsel of cake into his mouth like a ravenous child. I shook my head at him and handed him the coffee.

'What's up, beside the cruel and unusual punishment you're suffering?'

'We arrested Reg Dolan for the double murder of Lance Emerald and Wayne Dawson.'

I could feel my eyebrow raising.

'You did? That's a radical move, isn't it?'

'His DNA is on the scarf, and Jasmine told us he flew into a rage and threatened to kill Lance when he found out about Marge and him.'

'Jasmine?'

'On her first visit to the Pavilion to start her photographic assignment, she witnessed Delia visit Reg in his office. She heard him shouting and ranting about Lance later on the same morning. He wanted to kill Lance, but he didn't say why. She assumed Lance had done something annoying again. She didn't associate the two things, until we found Cracker dead as well. Then she interviewed Delia about Lance's death, and realised Lance had stolen Reg's girl, and ruined his career, so she came in to tell me.'

'You've got it all figured out then.'

'I knew I would. D.I. Antrim thinks he's such a big shot, but I'm the one with the experience.'

He tapped his head.

'And what does the DNA say?' I asked.

'The DNA?'

'Is Lance definitely Delia's father and Cracker's grandfather?'

'Obviously he is, but we're still waiting for the results. Aside from the DNA on the scarf, we also sent everyone's DNA in a batch and they're not finished analysing and comparing them all yet.'

'The results may surprise you. Our boy Lance got around a bit.'

'It won't make any difference. Reg is the murderer. Jealousy is a common motive, you should know that by now.'

I didn't reply. I felt deflated by George's confidence. Reg had not struck me as capable of murder. He had been devastated by Marge's desertion of him all those years ago, but he hadn't mentioned Lance to me in that respect. I found it odd. He had seemed more sad than cross. I couldn't associate him with a rage bad enough to kill one person, never mind two people. And why kill Cracker? The poor lad bore no responsibility for Lance's behaviour. It simply didn't add up.

'You're right of course,' I said.

'I'm glad you can see sense on this one. Now all we need is for you to come back to me. I'm still waiting for you to decide.'

I didn't dignify this statement with an answer. I had already told him several times that I had no intention of going back to him. After draining his coffee, George wrapped a second piece of cake in a napkin folding the corners in with care. I watched him with growing irritation until I could bear it no longer.

'That cake's not free, you know. I have to pay for it, and I make money on every slice.'

His eyes widened.

'Are you asking me to pay you?' he said, visibly shocked.

'The café is not a charity. I have to make a living too, you know.'

'I see Roz and Ghita having coffee in here all the time. Do you make them pay?'

'They work here for a pittance as a favour to me. Free coffee is a perk for them.'

'And not for me? I didn't realise how much you've changed. I don't deserve this.'

He stomped down the stairs casting resentful glances up at me, and almost falling down the last few when he missed his footing. I imagined the headlines; *Vengeful ex-wife shoves kind loving ex-husband down the stairs.* He slammed the door on the way out, leaving the bell jangling. I rolled my eyes. Sharon was so welcome to him.

I took a deep breath and dismissed him from my morning. My lovely objects from the cottage beckoned me with their novelty, and I soon forgot all about George and his unpleasant manner. When I had finished cleaning and organising, I put the door on the latch and strolled across the road to Surfusion carrying the Ganesha incense holder with me, wrapped in a piece of red tissue paper. Ghita saw me coming and came to the door, beaming. Her cheeks were rosy from the heat in the kitchen and she smelled of curry and spices.

'What a nice surprise,' she said. 'I think I see you less often now I work so close by.'

'Have you given up your job at the council,' I said, trying not to sound horrified.

'Not yet, but I reduced my hours for now. We're so busy trying to get ready for opening.'

'Are the boys here?'

'Yes, they're in the kitchen playing with the food.'

'I brought you a present.'

I took the red package out of my handbag and handed it to her.

'Oo. It's heavy. What is it?'

She unwrapped the tissue paper and examined the figure with wonder.

'Do you like it?'

'I love it. Where did you find him? He's so perfect. I can't believe it.'

She gave me a tight hug, and then gazed at the burner again shaking her head.

'We found it at the cottage of some hippies who have moved into assisted living. I guess they need a god of endings, not of beginnings.'

'Thank you so much. Ganesha will make all the difference. Can I show him to Kieron and Rohan?'

'Of course. But he's yours. You can lend him to the restaurant for good luck.'

She gave me another hug and ran into the kitchens squealing with delight. I contemplated following her, but my phone rang in my handbag and I scrabbled around trying to locate it. I managed to answer it before it rang off. Harry.

'Hello there, Ms Bowe. How do you fancy a trip to London? My cousin Tommy knows the detective who covered the Jimmy Dymond case.'

George could go to hell for all I cared. A lead is a lead.

'Great. When are we going?'

Chapter 34

Harry and I were back on the road early the next morning leaving Mouse with Olivia. Helen had gone back to see Martin again. He had not been pleased about them staying away longer. I found her immediate compliance unsettling. There was something about the way she reacted to his every whim that seemed unpleasantly familiar. Martin's control over Helen resembled George's former hold over me. What factor in our upbringing had made us so malleable? Probably the constant carping about what people might think and how a woman should behave. It's impossible for young women today to understand how hard it used to be to go against the grain. You had to be tough and independent, with a skin like a rhino, to break those unwritten rules about how to behave.

My career had happened by chance, but George never liked me being an investigative reporter. His colleagues made fun of him for having a missus with ideas above her station. He couldn't wait for me to get pregnant and give up my career. Even me having depression and losing my job was superior to being married to a feminist. He could understand his woman moping around the house like his mother better than if she had a trailblazing role in a TV show. The loss of the extra income had hit us hard, but secretly he felt vindicated.

'A penny for your thoughts,' said Harry.

'George told me Reg Dolan is under arrest for Lance's and Cracker's murders.'

'When did this happen?'

'Yesterday. He came to the shop to tell me. And to eat two pieces of cake without paying.'

'You sound grumpy. You should make him pay if you resent him eating your cake.'

'It's not the cake. It's the whole George thing. He's still expecting me to fall back into his arms. I'm so sick of having to tolerate him.'

'You don't have to.'

'But I do. He's Mouse's father. I don't have a right to alienate him. It's not fair on Mouse.'

'I guess it depends how much you care about the cake.'

'Not enough.'

I managed a smile.

'There you go. Maybe we should get engaged?'

I breathed in some saliva and choked on it, coughing and coughing until I thought my lungs would burst.

'What did you say?' I said, finally, when I had recovered.

'I was joking, sort of. But maybe it would persuade George to back off.'

I couldn't think of anything to say. When the divorce came through, I had sworn never to marry again. As far as I could tell, Harry hadn't asked me to marry him, but the panic I felt was real. I coughed again to play for time. He frowned at me.

'There's no need to act like I shot your dog. Forget it.'

'Don't be like that. You surprised me, that's all. I wasn't expecting a proposal.'

'It's not a proposal. When I propose, you'll know it.'

'Are you going to?'

'Not now.'

But he laughed and so did I. He put on some blues music and we sang along until we reached Tommy's warehouse a couple of hours later. Tommy emerged from his tatty office which was tacked on to the side of the warehouse as an afterthought. I noticed his jumper had less holes than usual and his jeans appeared clean. I presumed our visit to see D.S. Morris had something to do with his attempt at style. Harry laughed at him.

'You didn't have to dress up for Tanya, you know she's not interested.'

'And who told you that?' I said. 'Hello Tommy.'

I gave him a hug for one second too long, just to annoy Harry. Tommy smirked afterwards, as if he had a secret. We unloaded the van and Tommy gave Harry a scribbled receipt for the goods. Their system only made sense to themselves and I never asked Harry about it fearing he wouldn't appreciate being quizzed. When we had finished, Tommy called D.S. Morris from the landline in his office. He put his hand over the receiver.

'Old school,' he said. 'No mobile phone.'

D.S. Morris came to the door of his terraced house in Greenwich in his slippers with a pipe clamped between his teeth. He wore a cardigan buttoned up almost to his neck and a pair of baggy tweed trousers. His dark eyes twinkled in their sockets as he anticipated talking about an old case. I noticed a battered folder sitting on the dining table and the hairs on my arms stood on end. My excitement lasted thirty seconds. D.S. Morris turned his gaze on me and rubbed his chin.

'Can you make us some tea, love?' he said. 'We're going to talk policing.'

I waited for Harry or Tommy to say something, but the silence persisted. I rolled my eyes at Harry and stomped out to the kitchen where I crashed the mugs onto the tray and generally made a lot of noise. I ransacked the place for biscuits and found a tin of Danish butter cookies in the cupboard, still sealed and obviously being saved for a 'special' occasion. In a petty act of revenge, I pulled the tape off and opened the tin. First, I ate a couple of biscuits myself to prevent resealing of the tin, and then I put the pot of tea, the milk and the mugs on a tray with the opened tin, and barged my way back into the sitting room. The three men were sitting at the table reviewing the contents of the folder. They looked up as I entered. I saw D.S. Morris's eyes flicker to the tin. His eyebrows knitted together, but he did not comment. I gave a large fake smile.

'Tea's up, gents.'

'Great,' said Harry. 'Come and join us. D.S. Morris has the original folder from the investigation. He's got photos and everything.'

I heard the note of entreaty in his voice and took pity on him. After all, the old dinosaur Morris had come up trumps for us when he didn't know us from Adam. I even felt slightly embarrassed about opening his precious tin of biscuits. I placed the tray on the table and went through the pantomime of pouring tea and adding milk and sugar to the mugs. I handed round the tin of biscuits and everyone took their favourites. Soon the papers from the file were dusted in buttery crumbs. I sat beside Tommy and he handed me some papers to peruse.

'Now that we've all got our tea,' said Morris. 'I'll tell you what I know about the whole sorry affair. For a start, Lance Emerald never called himself that while he stayed in London. We all knew him as Jimmy Dymond. He didn't have much to recommend him, but he sure could sing. His talent meant he quickly got picked up by the club circuit, especially the private clubs. They were run, in the most part by wide boys associated with London gangster families like the Richards and the Edwards. Jimmy made himself indispensable to the boss of the Edwards family.'

'So that guaranteed his gigs.'

'Exactly. However, Jimmy always took an extreme interest in the ladies. He went through a string of them in a short time. The bouncers on the doors told me he left with a different girl every night.'

'That sounds like our guy,' I said.

'Well, Edwards had a daughter, Susan. She was the apple of his eye. A real looker. Blonde hair, blue eyes, big boobies (here he made a gesture with his hands and they all laughed). You know the sort of thing. Anyway, Jimmy couldn't take his eyes off her and started to court her in secret. I can't imagine what she saw in him, but what do I know?'

'Wasn't he taking a massive risk,' said Tommy. 'Playing house with the boss's daughter?'

'That's just it. The idiot got her pregnant. When Edwards found out, he took out a hit on Jimmy, who found out in time to flee to France, taking a suitcase of money he stole from Edwards's nightclub.'

'What happened to Susan?' I said.

'Jimmy dumped her when he left the country. I didn't find out for years what happened next. Her father forced her to marry one of his henchmen, and she had the baby, but she became a drug addict and overdosed soon afterwards.'

'What happened to the baby?' said Harry.

'I don't know.'

'What sex was it?' I said.

'I never found out. Edwards drank himself to death and his wife died of emphysema from smoking. I have no idea what happened to the baby.'

'Maybe Susan's husband kept it. Do you know his name?'

'I'm sorry. I have no idea.'

We sat in silence after that. I looked at the other papers from the folder. There were clippings from the Evening Standard with a photograph of Lance Emerald standing beside a glowering giant of a man who smiled in a way which suggested he hadn't had much practice. I stared at the photograph willing it to tell me something I didn't already know. Then I saw a female hand on Lance/Jimmy's shoulder and I remembered Jasmine's photo of Lance. The photograph had been cropped. Could this be a photograph of Susan Edwards? Would she look like any cast member of the Tribute show? There was no way of knowing if this was a red herring. I had to follow it up. My spider senses were tingling, as Mouse would have said. I took a snap with my mobile phone to have something to use as a guide for Mouse.

'How come Edwards didn't hunt Jimmy down in France?' I said.

'I'm guessing he didn't use that name. Edwards didn't speak French. He couldn't operate over there,' said Morris.

'So, Jimmy changed his name back to Lance Emerald?' said Harry.

'That's why nobody knows what happened in London. Except Lance,' I said. 'And, maybe, his child.'

'That's a pretty good motive for murder right there,' said Harry.

'But how will you find the child?' said Tommy.

'DNA,' I said. 'The police in Seacastle have tested everyone who has been involved with the Pavilion theatre show. If Susan and Lance's child has returned for revenge, they'll show up in the DNA.'

'It would help if we knew what she looked like,' said Harry.

'I think we can find out,' I said. 'We need to search the files for the original photographs from this article in the Evening Standard. I have a contact who used to work for the paper.'

D.S. Morris narrowed his eyes and stared at me.

'I misjudged you,' he said. 'I'm old fashioned, but I'm not stupid. If I can help with the case, I'm at your service.'

'I'm sorry about the biscuits,' I said. 'That was very childish of me.'

'I'd completely forgotten about the tin. Good job you found them. I love a nice biscuit. Good luck with the case. My instinct would be to leave well alone, but I guess there's an innocent man being held for these murders.'

'Thanks. We'll let Tommy know how it goes,' I said.

He tamped his pipe with new tobacco and lit it again. We all stood up to leave and he waved from the table.

'Good hunting,' he said.

On our way home from London, I called the editor of the local paper, one of my contacts from *Uncovering the Truth*. He used to work for the Evening Standard on the gossip columns and knew where all the bodies were buried.

'Tanya? Are you back on the trail? I didn't realise they were filming a new series.'

'Definitely not. Can I ask you a small favour for old time's sake?'

'After what you did for me covering the competition? I owe you a large favour, not a small one.'

'I need a copy of a photograph published in the Evening Standard in nineteen-ninety-two or three. Where's the best place to look for it?'

'That would be the Getty Images site. They purchased the archive from the newspaper and have all the originals. You can peruse for free, but they charge you an arm and a leg to buy one.'

'Thanks, Joe.'

'Thank you, Tanya. I'm so grateful. Gotta go.'

He hung up, leaving me slightly puzzled that he would still be so grateful about our days collaborating on Uncovering the Truth. I shrugged and turned to Harry.

'Joe says we can use the Getty Images site to track down the photo of Lance. Since we have the approximate timings of Lance's transgressions, Mouse can use his skills to search the archives.'

'Great. Fancy fish and chips for supper? You can't want to cook after the day we've had.'

'You always have the best ideas.'

Chapter 35

The next morning, Flo called me at the Grotty Hovel, her voice high with excitement.

'Can I come over and talk to you? The DNA results are in, and there were some surprises. I thought you might be able to help me with their significance before I gave them to George. I want to be sure we are understanding what they are telling us.'

'And you're not sure he will listen?'

'Unfortunately. You know what he's like.'

'I have some new information on the case which I haven't told him yet. He asked me to back off, now he's got rid of Antrim.'

'The ungrateful toad. I'll be there in an hour or two. I've got a draft report to write first.'

I woke Mouse and asked him to open the Vintage and deal with the lunchtime regulars, while I sorted through the new information I had on the case. I did not tell him about Flo coming over, or he would have wanted to stay at home. I gave him instructions about using the Getty Images site to search for the photograph and I forwarded him the snap I had taken of the article in D.S. Morris's file. The photograph app on my mobile phone still contained the snap I'd taken of Lance Emerald's dressing room in the Pavilion. My finger hovered over the delete button, but the tatty dressing table and the coat hooks were like a sad still life invoking Lances last days. I stared at the photograph which seemed to be missing something I couldn't put my finger on.

Mouse left for the shop after a shower, muttering about his right to eight hours sleep, and exploitation of the working classes. I kissed the top of his head and told him to stop being so dramatic. Then I organised the information I had on the case into lists. It became clear to me that there were two vital pieces of evidence which tied the threads of the case together. The first was Mouse's Brighton and Hove Albion scarf. I made a timeline for it from when he lost it at the Shanty through to the moment it had been found on Lance's neck. Delia had taken it from the Shanty and lost it at the Pavilion where it turned up on a hook in Lance's dressing room at the time of Jasmine's photo of Lance. Somebody had then used it to strangle Lance.

The second piece of evidence was the ring given to Jimmy Dymond, Lance's real name, by Frank Sinatra. Lance wore it to the Pavilion because he wanted to enjoy it before he died. It had been front and centre in Jasmine's portrait of Lance which was published in the local paper, meaning that it's presence on Lance's finger was no secret. Wayne 'Cracker' Dawson had claimed that Lance had given him the ring for Marge. Whoever had murdered Cracker had stolen the ring from him, so it had either economical or sentimental value for the murderer.

I paced around the sitting room, trying to make sense of the clues. I had almost worn a path into the new rug from our clearance in Chichester by the time Flo rang the doorbell. I opened the door and welcomed her in. She wore her opera singer's cloak and dramatic black velvet dress as if coming to a state funeral, but her eyes were merry. She gave me an exuberant hug and swept her cloak off her shoulders, knocking over the coat stand, and causing momentary chaos as Hades shot around the room before diving into his laundry basket.

'Sorry it took me so long to arrive. You won't believe any of this,' she said, letting me pick up the coats, as she took out her computer. 'Lance Emerald is not Cracker's grandfather, but he is related to other people in the cast, and he wasn't the only person spreading his seed around the theatres of England.'

I let out a whistle as I tried to compute.

'Holy crap. That's put the cat among the pigeons.'

I looked at my watch and was stunned to find the morning gone and the hands pointing at past one o'clock. I needed a stimulant before tackling such a revelation.

'Let's make a large pot of coffee and some sandwiches as I suspect we will need all our brain cells on full power.'

Soon we were sitting on the same side of the dining table, with a stack of ham and cheese croissants, and a steaming pot of coffee on a mat to the side of us, gazing at Flo's screen. Excitement and caffeine coursed through my bloodstream. Flo opened an Excel sheet with multiple columns. I couldn't make head or tail of it.

'What are we looking at?' I said.

'Let's start with the Dawsons. Cracker's DNA is a mixture of Delia's and another unnamed man. The revelation is that Delia's DNA shows she is the daughter of Marge Dawson and Reg Dolan.'

'Reg? Oh heavens. He'll be made up. Delia told him Lance Emerald was her father. Maybe that family will have some sort of a happy ending after all. I hope Marge will give Reg a chance now.'

'Who knows? It's a good thing we have DNA to tell the truth for us.'

'Especially in this case,' I said.

'And then there's Hunter. He's the son of Cynthia Walters and Reg Dolan.'

'Reg again? And we thought Lance was the profligate one. Reg is in for a big surprise.'

Flo laughed.

'Some people discover they have a child late in life. But not many discover they have two, by two different women. Anyway, the piece de resistance is this DNA which we haven't identified yet. Lance Emerald is the father, but her mother is a mystery.'

'A daughter? But where did this DNA come from?'

'The scarf.'

'How many people left DNA on the scarf?'

'Um, let me see. Delia, Lance (obviously), Reg, Mouse and the unknown female.'

'What about the whisky bottle?'

'They took several sets of fingerprints from it. Lance, Cracker and the unknown female. But the person who added Rohypnol may not have touched the bottle.'

'Or may have worn gloves. What about the basement? Were there any revelations from there?'

Flo scrolled down the page.

'Whoever killed Cracker needed half an hour for the Rohypnol to kick in. I suspect they had a drink first, or a coffee somewhere, and then they lured him to the basement with the promise of something.'

'Sex?'

'Maybe. The DNA we found in the basement comes from Cynthia, Hunter, Olivia and the unknown female.'

'So, the mystery woman's DNA is at both murder scenes?'

'It looks like it. Does that fit with your new information?'

'It does. We discovered Lance spent the early 90s in London on the private club circuit. He hung around with some of the gangsters running them, and managed to get the daughter of one of the bosses pregnant. He then ran off to France where he spent twenty years on the party circuit in Monaco. Apparently, he discovered he had cancer recently and decided to come home.'

'That didn't work out well for him, did it?'

'I don't know. Dying of lung cancer isn't a picnic, maybe being strangled while drugged saved him from a worse fate.'

'But why kill Wayne Dawson? He didn't contribute much to society, but it seems over the top to kill him, even if you thought he was Lance's grandson.'

'Are you sure it was the same murderer?'

'No, but it seems likely. Female murderers are not common, but it happens,' said Flo.

'I suppose when you've killed once, the second time is easier. Do you have a list of the people from whom you took DNA samples?'

'Hang on. I'll bring it up.'

I took a swig of coffee and reviewed the list on the screen. There were a surprising number of people in the theatre for both murders and the police had also taken Marge and Delia's DNA for elimination purposes. I scanned up and down hoping for inspirations. My mobile phone rang, and I tutted and rolled my eyes at Flo.

'Honestly, how important can it be?' I said, and switched it to silent. 'I need to concentrate here.'

I pushed the phone away from me and tried to refocus on the list. But then my gut tightened and I pulled it towards me again.

'What's up,' said Flo. 'You've gone pale.'

'Give me a second. There's something I've got to check.'

I felt sick as I opened the photograph app and returned to the snap of the dressing room. No scarf hung from the hooks on the wall. Anyway, I would've noticed it if it had been in the dressing room. The scarf has bright blue and white stripes and it would have been totally out of place. But I didn't. So that meant the scarf had been in the dressing room when Jasmine took her photograph of Lance, but not afterwards when I interviewed him. I breathed out slowly to try and calm myself.

'Is Jasmine Smith on the list,' I said.

'Of DNA samples? No. Who's she?'

'That's exactly what I'm thinking. I've been working with her on articles for the local paper. She asked me to write short life stories for the contestants in the competition. She told me she had a contract with the paper and offered me a generous fee.'

'That does not sound like the Worthing Echo. They're broke. They manage to stagger on, due to a grant from the council.'

I sighed and held up my hand. I dialled Joe at the Echo and waited for him to answer.

'Hi Tanya. Twice in a week. What did I do to deserve it?'

'I have a question for you about the Tribute competition.'

'Shoot.'

'How much are you paying Jasmine to produce the articles about the contestants?'

'Paying her? I thought the articles were free. I can't afford to pay for them. What am I going to do?'

'It's okay, Joe. You won't be paying anything. I just needed to check. I've got to go.'

I hung up. A memory of the expensive clothes and designer shoes she wore into my shop on the first day we worked together hit me and I gasped.

'You're scaring me now,' said Flo. 'What's happening?'

'It's her,' I said. 'Jasmine. Her name isn't Smith either. It might be Edwards. She's the result of a liaison between Lance Emerald and an East End gangster's daughter. He dumped her mother, who committed suicide by overdosing on drugs.'

'How do you know that?'

'I met the police officer who covered the area in 1992. Mouse is looking for a photograph of her mother right now.'

'Maybe that's why he rang you?'

I grabbed my phone and checked my messages. Sure enough, a message from Mouse remained unopened. *Can't get into Getty Images without a password. Have called Jasmine who is going to come over and help me, as she has a subscription.* My blood ran cold and I stood up, grabbing my handbag.

'Where are we going?' said Flo.

'Second Home. Mouse has invited the murderer to look at photographs, to find one of her mother.'

'Text him a warning.'

'I just did. Let's go. She's already killed twice. Who says she's going to stop at two? Can you please ring George while we're driving there?'

'It would be better if you tell him and I drive. You're quicker than me. I'll follow you in to the shop after I've parked the car.'

'Okay. Let's go.'

Chapter 36

I'm not sure how many red lights we drove through on the way to Second Home. As usual they seemed to conspire against us. Flo huffed and puffed but she is a skilful driver and drove through the smallest holes in the traffic. My adrenaline had hit nauseous levels and I struggled to remain calm. The shop seemed further away than the moon, although it took us under ten minutes to get there. I couldn't help imagining horrible scenarios if we arrived too late. I would never forgive myself if she harmed Mouse. Never.

When we were almost there, Flo stopped on the last corner before the shop, admonishing me to act normally and get Mouse out of there. I jumped out of the car sprinting to the door. I let out a couple of deep breaths before I entered, forcing myself to breathe normally and smiling as I entered. The bell jangled in my ear like a fire alarm. Downstairs looked deserted and the dust on the table tops had not been disturbed by curious fingers. The glass fishing floats swayed in the breeze which came uninvited into the shop with me.

I called out a cheery greeting and I felt panic rise in my gullet when it echoed around the shop. Then, I heard Mouse.

'I'm up here with Jasmine,' he said. 'We're looking at photographs from the Evening Standard.'

Clever boy. He meant to warn me that the gig was up. They had obviously found the photograph and recognised Jasmine's mother with Lance. I swore to myself never to ignore my phone again, or put it on silent.

'You'd better come up,' said Jasmine, her voice oddly mechanical.

I glanced out of the window and down the street towards the police station, but I couldn't see George's car. He had sounded extremely distressed when he realised Mouse might be in danger, and promised me he would be there as fast as he could. It took me a few hysterical sentences to get through to him, but once I had, he told me to wait for him outside. I know I should have, but I couldn't leave Mouse alone with that woman. Maybe I could appeal to her humanity, if she had any left.

I climbed the stairs and entered the café. Mouse and Jasmine were seated at the window table with Jasmine's laptop in front of them. Two empty tea cups had been pushed to one side. How long had she been in the shop with Mouse? His face had gone pale and the look he gave me betrayed his fear. An icy chill ran up my back. I smiled at Jasmine as if I hadn't a care in the world.

'I thought I'd find you both up here. It's really great of you to help Mouse,' I said. 'He's doing some research for me on Lance Emerald's time in London, but he needs to

239

leave now, because George is taking him to the cinema. Why don't I sit with you instead?'

Jasmine narrowed her eyes. I could almost see her calculating our respective values. She obviously thought Mouse the prize.

'I'm afraid he can't leave now. We've just got to the interesting part, haven't we, Mouse?'

Mouse's expression looked odd and his eyes were half-closed. To my horror, I realised she had drugged him. And I already knew what she had intended to do next. My vision clouded as an unnatural fury seized hold of me, and time seemed to stand still as I launched myself at her. I had a millisecond to register the surprise on her face as I landed on the table, knocking her expensive computer and the two cups and saucers to the ground with a crash. Pieces of china flew everywhere and the screen broke, as I scrabbled with her.

'Get out of here,' I shouted at Mouse, as I slapped Jasmine with all my might. He stumbled to his feet, and almost fell backwards. Momentarily distracted, I grabbed his arm to stop him falling into the window. Jasmine tugged at my hair and tried to pull me off her, but I hit her again and again in rage and fear. Finally, she whimpered her surrender and I tried to stand up. I screamed abuse at her and shook with anger. I felt strong hands encircle my waist, and someone lifted me off her still shouting and kicking.

'It's okay, Tan. I'm here. You can stop now. Mouse is safe.'

George pulled me away. P.C. Brennan appeared out of nowhere and put handcuffs on Jasmine as he read her rights. She glared at me; her face puffy from the onslaught of slaps I had aimed at her. I looked around. George's calm face told me everything would be okay. I went limp in his arms for a moment and enjoyed the familiar feel and smell of my ex-husband for a last time as he comforted me. When I had recovered sufficiently, I approached Mouse, who had taken refuge with Flo. She mussed his hair and whispered sweet nothings in his ear that made him blush.

'Are you all right, darling? I'm so sorry,' I said.

'Sorry for what? I used to think She-ra was pretty great until I saw you in action.'

He giggled softly. His eyes looked droopy, but I guessed the dosage had been counteracted by the adrenaline in his body. The police cordoned off the Vintage while they collected evidence, and P.C. Brennan took our statements. George beckoned me to the back of the shop while Mouse told him everything he could remember.

'I've had quite a day,' he said. 'I'm feeling really upset.'

'Your day? What about mine? Are you completely insensitive?'

'You have no idea. None at all.'

I sighed.

'What could be worse than a mad woman trying to kill your son? Did they fire you?'

'No, it's much worse than that. It's Sharon.'

'She hasn't left you?'

'It's worse than that. She's pregnant and she wants to get married.'

'Pregnant. Holy crap, George. I thought that would be good news.'

'So did I. But now I'm not sure anymore. I planned to leave her, but I can't abandon her.'

'Maybe you'll change your mind. Having a baby together is bonding.'

George frowned and shook his head. I don't know how I would have coped with this news if Harry hadn't turned up almost immediately after George's revelation. He gave George a hug and congratulated him, and said all the right things. I had turned to stone with shock. The events of the afternoon had dealt me a double blow. It wasn't that I minded about Sharon being pregnant, giving George what he had always wanted, but his obvious horror at the news had shocked me. That on top of the Jasmine thing made me long to be home with my man, my stepson and my cat.

While Mouse finished his interview, I gave Harry strict instructions not to spill the beans about the baby. It was George's news to share, and it looked as if he had decided not to do it then. Mouse came over looking less groggy and I patted George on the back and handed a set of keys to the shop to the forensic team. Harry drove us back to the Grotty Hovel where Flo transferred to her own vehicle, and drove home, being far too civilized to intrude on our reunion.

Chapter 37

We stopped on the way home to buy a takeaway and sent Mouse next door to rescue Olivia who was languishing by herself with Helen still away. I gave him strict instructions not to mention the afternoon's events, as I felt we needed a normal family meal without mention of murders. We could tell her the truth in the morning if she hadn't already found out from her phone and whatever social media outlets she used. Then she could ask all the questions she wanted to. I found the fact that Helen had not returned from ministering to Martin a little strange. She had been desperate to get back to support Olivia through the final days of the competition.

Mouse returned from next door with a sulky Olivia who seemed depressed. She had seemed extra preoccupied in recent days. I wondered if her rehearsals had not gone well. I pretended not to notice the black cloud hovering over her and be my normal jolly self.

'How's your mum?' I said. 'Still annoying?'

To my chagrin, her lip quivered and she seemed close to tears. Mouse put an arm around her shoulders and brushed her hair out of her eyes.

'What's wrong?' he said. 'Was Hunter nasty to you again?'

She shook her head.

'I'm worried about Mum. She wanted to come back to Seacastle today but Dad won't let her leave the house. He's been acting really weird lately and he's…'

'He's what?' I said.

'I think he hit her. I'm not sure. It's just…'

'Hit her?' I said. 'I can't believe it.'

My heart dropped in my ribcage, and I flashed a glance of complete panic at Harry. Olivia bit her lip and swallowed.

'Well, I'm not sure exactly, but he's been shouting at her a lot and staying out late at night and, and, and I found a receipt for a restaurant in his pocket when he said he'd been at the office. I didn't mean to. I wanted to use his credit card to buy something and it fell out.'

'Did you tell your mother?' I said.

'No, but she thinks he wants to get rid of her.'

'I'll tell you what,' I said, trying to keep my voice calm. 'I'll drive up there tomorrow and bring her back down to Seacastle. She can't miss the show.'

'Why don't we both drive up there right now?' said Harry, taking out his keys. 'No time like the present.'

He had gone pale and the muscles on his cheeks had bunched up. I knew he had added two and two together and made five, just like me.

'We can take my car,' I said. 'The Mini needs a fast trip to clean her pipes. Olivia, will you stay here with Mouse tonight? I don't want either of you to be alone.'

'We'll be okay,' said Mouse. 'We've got Hades. He's more dangerous than any guard dog.'

I grabbed a packet of chips and sprinkled them with salt. Harry smiled when he saw me stuffing them into a bag.

'You would have been great in the army,' he said and squeezed my arm.

'Put the left overs in the fridge when you've had enough,' I said to Mouse and Olivia. 'We'll be back soon.'

Olivia gave me a damp smile. I managed not to cry until we were outside on the pavement. Harry put his arms around me and held me close while I wept.

'I'm afraid,' I said. 'What if he has hurt her, or—'

'Don't say that. We'll be there soon. Get in the car.'

I tried not to break the speed limit on my way to their house, but my agitation increased every time I had to slow down. Harry fed me on chips and tried to take my mind off the reason we were on the road.

'I've made a decision,' he said.

'You're not going to propose again, are you?'

'No, you silly Moo. About my brother. I see how much you care about Helen, despite your differences. I'm going to go to Devon and see him. Life is cruel. You never know when you'll see someone for the last time. I can't let ancient history come between us.'

'Is that a dig at me?'

'No. You love your sister. It shows. You need to appreciate her more. She is a pretty special person. Just rather different to you.'

'Chalk and cheese.'

'Fish and chips, but they go pretty well together, don't they?'

I sighed.

'Do you think he's going to hurt her?'

'I don't know. But we can't leave her there. It sounds like he's found someone else and is taking it out on Helen. Men have murdered for less. We need to get her out of there.'

'And I thought George was bad. I had no idea she had problems. She always talked about mine. We never talked about hers. I guess I thought she didn't have any. I was jealous.'

'And now?'

'I'm trying to stick to the speed limit despite my heart thundering in my chest.'

We arrived at Helen and Martin's house at about nine-thirty and parked opposite the front door. The curtains were drawn in the sitting room, but shards of light escaped into the front garden. Harry put his hand on mine.

'Stay calm. Whatever happens, stay calm. Okay? If it gets physical, you grab Helen and leave Martin to me.'

'Understood.'

'Let's go get our girl.'

We walked up the path to the front door, the gravel crunching under our feet. I wondered if they could hear it. I felt sick with worry. Why couldn't we hear voices? Had he done something to her? I rang the doorbell. After a short time, I saw Martin's silhouette coming up the hall. The door opened and he peered out at us. His brow wrinkled as he tried and failed to compute.

'Tanya. What are you doing here? And who's this?'

'I'm Harry Fletcher, a friend of Tanya's.'

'We were just passing, so we thought we'd stop and pick Helen up. Olivia's so nervous about the competition with all the weird stuff that's been going on. She needs her mother.'

Martin did not move from the doorway.

'Helen's asleep.'

'Wake her up,' said Harry.

I knew that tone. Martin's eyes widened. He was tall, but weedy, no match for Harry at his inflated best. But he didn't move.

'I don't know who this guy is, but I don't like his tone. I've no intention of waking Helen,' he said.

'Please, Martin. Olivia needs her.'

At that time, I had no idea how damaged their marriage had become, but I knew Olivia had always been the true love of his life. He would never hurt her on purpose. He sighed and turned on his heel. I followed him into the house. Helen lay on the sofa, sound asleep. I thought it odd, considering the hour, but I wouldn't yield. I shook her quite roughly in my anxiety. She opened her eyes and smiled at me in a woozy way.

'Hello, Tan Tan. What are you doing in my dream?'

'We're going to take you back to Seacastle to see Olivia. She's missing you.'

'Oh.'

Her eyes closed again and I realised she had taken a sleeping pill, or had been fed one. I felt panic in the pit of my stomach.

'Can you carry her?' I said to Harry.

'Sure,' said Harry. 'No need to wake her. She can sleep on the back seat. Before you know it, we'll be home.'

'I won't let you take her,' said Martin, moving to block the sitting room door.

'I think you will,' said Harry.

The steel edge to his voice made the hairs on my neck stand on end. Martin hesitated, until Harry took a pace towards him. Then he backed away with his hands up.

'Okay, okay. Can't you take a joke? She's all yours.'

Harry picked Helen up with one swift movement and carried her rapidly to the front door. He waited for me to catch up with him.

'I don't want her back,' said Martin.

'You won't get the choice,' I said.

Chapter 38

We drove home at a more sensible pace. Helen snored softly on the back seat, hidden under an old picnic blanket covered in hairs from Hades. I felt nauseous from the amount of adrenaline still swirling around in my blood stream. I wasn't sure how much more danger I could take in one day. I felt as if someone had run over me with a steamroller and then backed up to be sure. I reviewed the clues Helen had left me about her marriage melting down, but they were not solid enough to form the basis for any conclusions.

She had, as usual, displayed a stiff upper lip and hidden all her problems from me. When we were little, she always protected me and took the blame for many of my transgressions. We had lost the knack of getting on as we grew up as her 'older and better' act had started to grate on me. But now I saw that even her support of George had been an act of protection. She didn't understand depression, but she had decided I couldn't be on my own to cope with it.

'Feeling calmer?' said Harry. 'You were terrific back there. Martin wilted when you mentioned Olivia.'

'What about you? Helen's quite robust, but you picked her up as if she were a sylph.'

'I'm not robust,' muttered Helen.

I laughed.

'You're supposed to be asleep,' I said.

'I am asleep,' she said.

You can't talk about Helen, even when she's asleep. She has ears like sonar detectors. Sometimes I think she has bat genes.

'She is a little plump,' said Harry, winking at me.

'I can still hear you.'

'Go back to sleep. I promise we won't talk about you anymore,' I said.

Harry stroked my cheek, and I thanked George in my head for gifting me this special man. If George had not thrown me out of our house, I would not have met Harry outside the Grotty Hovel. Thank goodness I didn't use a mobile phone then. I might have been looking at it and missed him arrive. Sliding doors.

We had a quick journey back to Seacastle and were home before midnight. A full moon shone into our street defeating the streetlamps with its brightness. There was even a parking space right outside the Grotty Hovel. A rather groggy Helen came into the house with us. She was immediately enveloped by an ecstatic Olivia, who jumped off the couch where she had been watching a movie with Mouse and Hades.

'Mummy. You're back.'

'Did you miss me?'

'More than all the stars in the sky.'

'That's nice,' said Helen, her voice breaking.

My eyes filled with tears too, and I had to turn away to hide my emotion. Harry had a bad habit of always being right. I had been spoiled and silly, and I nearly lost my sister because she only focused on my problems and not on hers. I didn't intend for that to ever happen again.

Once everyone else had gone to bed, I sat on the sofa with Harry and kissed him passionately in the moonlight, which crept into the sitting room and made us look like silver statues. His strong arms felt like a fortress around my heart. The horror of the day slowly dimmed and was quenched by the power of the moonlight. Harry sighed with contentment and stroked my hair. I gazed into his eyes and floated on a cloud of love. I felt light and free and cocooned by his feelings for me. My fear of losing Helen had made me realise just how much I loved him too. He stared back at me, reading my intense emotions with ease, and he smiled at me.

'You're my woman,' he said. 'And I'm your man.'

'Don't ever leave me, Harry Fletcher.'

'Never. I promise.'

Thank you for reading my book. Please leave me a review if you enjoyed it.

You can pre-order the next in series
– TOXIC VOWS –
On Amazon

Other books

The Seacastle Mysteries - a cosy mystery series set on the south coast of England

Deadly Return (Book 1)

Staying away is hard, but returning may prove fatal. Tanya Bowe, a former investigative journalist, is adjusting to life as an impoverished divorcee in the seaside town of Seacastle. She crosses paths with a long-lost schoolmate, Melanie Conrad, during a house clearance to find stock for her vintage shop. The two women renew their friendship, but their reunion takes a tragic turn when Mel is found lifeless at the foot of the stairs in the same house.

While the police are quick to label Mel's death as an accident, Tanya's gut tells her there's more to the story. Driven by her instincts, she embarks on her own investigation, delving into Mel's mysterious past. As she probes deep into the Conrad family's secrets, Tanya uncovers a complex web of lies and blackmail. But the further she digs, the more intricate the puzzle becomes. As Tanya's determination grows, so does the shadow of danger. Each new revelation brings her closer to a chilling truth. Can she unravel the secrets surrounding Mel's demise before the killer strikes again?

Eternal Forest (Book 2)

What if proving a friend's husband innocent of murder implicates her instead?

Tanya Bowe, an ex-investigative journalist, and divorcee, runs a vintage shop in the coastal town of Seacastle. When her old friend, Lexi Burlington-Smythe borrows the office above the shop as a base for the campaign to create a kelp sanctuary off the coast, Tanya is thrilled with the chance to get involved and make some extra money. Tanya soon gets drawn into the high-stake arguments surrounding the campaign, as tempers are frayed, and her friends, Roz and Ghita favour opposing camps. When a celebrity eco warrior is murdered, the evidence implicates Roz's husband Ed, and Tanya finds her loyalties stretched to breaking point as she struggles to discover the true identity of the murderer.

Toxic Vows (Book 4)
Coming soon.

Other books by the Author

I write under various pen names in different genres. If you are looking for another mystery, why don't you try **Mortal Mission,** written as Pip Skinner.

Mortal Mission
Will they find life on Mars, or death?

When the science officer for the first crewed mission to Mars dies suddenly, backup Hattie Fredericks gets the coveted place on the crew. But her presence on the Starship provokes suspicion when it coincides with a series of incidents which threaten to derail the mission.

After a near-miss while landing on the planet, the world watches as Hattie and her fellow astronauts struggle to survive. But, worse than the harsh elements on Mars, is their growing realisation that someone, somewhere, is trying to destroy the mission.

When more astronauts die, Hattie doesn't know who to trust. And her only allies are 35 million miles away. As the tension ratchets up, violence and suspicion invade both worlds. If you like science-based sci-fi and a locked-room mystery with a twist, you'll love this book.

The Green Family Saga

Rebel Green – Book 1

Relationships fracture when two families find themselves caught up in the Irish Troubles.

The Green family move to Kilkenny from England in 1969, at the beginning of the conflict in Northern Ireland. They rent a farmhouse on the outskirts of town, and make friends with the O'Connor family next door. Not every member of the family adapts easily to their new life, and their differing approaches lead to misunderstandings and friction. Despite this, the bonds between the family members deepen with time.

Perturbed by the worsening violence in the North threatening to invade their lives, the children make a pact never to let the troubles come between them. But promises can be broken, with tragic consequences for everyone.

Africa Green – Book 2

Will a white chimp save its rescuers or get them killed?

Journalist Isabella Green travels to Sierra Leone, a country emerging from civil war, to write an article about a chimp sanctuary. Animals that need saving are her obsession, and she can't resist getting involved with the project, which is on the verge of bankruptcy. She forms a bond with local boy, Ten, and army veteran, Pete, to try and save it. When they rescue a rare white chimp from a village frequented by a dangerous rebel splinter group, the resulting media interest could save the sanctuary. But the rebel group have not signed the cease fire. They believe the voodoo power of the white chimp protects them from bullets, and they are determined to take it back so they can storm the capital. When Pete and Ten go missing, only Isabella stands in the rebels' way. Her love for the chimps unlocks the fighting spirit within her. Can she save the sanctuary or will she die trying?

Fighting Green – Book 3

Liz Green is desperate for a change. The Dot-Com boom is raging in the City of London, and she feels exhausted and out of her depth. Added to that, her long-term boyfriend, Sean O'Connor, is drinking too much and shows signs of going off the rails. Determined to start anew, Liz abandons both Sean and her job, and buys a near-derelict house in Ireland to renovate.

She moves to Thomastown where she renews old ties and makes new ones, including two lawyers who become rivals for her affection. When Sean's attempt to win her back goes disastrously wrong, Liz finishes with him for good. Finding herself almost penniless, and forced to seek new ways to survive, Liz is torn between making a fresh start and going back to her old loves.

Can Liz make a go of her new life, or will her past become her future?

The Sam Harris Series (written as PJ Skinner)

Set in the late 1980's and through the 1990's, the thrilling Sam Harris Adventure series navigates through the career of a female geologist. Themes such as women working in formerly male domains, and what constitutes a normal existence, are developed in the context of Sam's constant ability to find herself in the middle of an adventure or mystery. Sam's home life provides a contrast to her adventures and feeds her need to escape. Her attachment to an unfaithful boyfriend is the thread running through her romantic life, and her attempts to break free of it provide another side to her character.

The first book in the Sam Harris Series sets the scene for the career of an unwilling heroine, whose bravery and resourcefulness are needed to navigate a series of adventures set in remote sites in Africa and South America. Based loosely on the real-life adventures of the author, the settings and characters are given an authenticity that will connect with readers who enjoy adventure fiction and mysteries set in remote settings with realistic scenarios.

Fool's Gold - Book 1

Newly qualified geologist Sam Harris is a woman in a man's world - overlooked, underpaid but resilient and passionate. Desperate for her first job, and nursing a broken heart, she accepts an offer from notorious entrepreneur Mike Morton, to search for gold deposits in the remote rainforests of Sierramar. With the help of nutty local heiress, Gloria Sanchez, she soon settles into life in Calderon, the capital. But when she accidentally uncovers a long-lost clue to a treasure buried deep within the jungle, her journey really begins. Teaming up with geologist Wilson Ortega, historian Alfredo Vargas and the mysterious Don Moises, they venture through the jungle, where she lurches between excitement and insecurity. Yet there is a far graver threat looming; Mike and Gloria discover that one of the members of the expedition is plotting to seize the fortune for himself and is willing to do anything to get it. Can Sam survive and find the treasure or will her first adventure be her last?

Hitler's Finger - Book 2

The second book in the Sam Harris Series sees the return of our heroine Sam Harris to Sierramar to help her friend Gloria track down her boyfriend, the historian, Alfredo Vargas. Geologist Sam Harris loves getting her hands dirty. So, when she learns that her friend Alfredo has gone missing in Sierramar, she gives her personal life some much needed space and hops on the next plane.

But she never expected to be following the trail of a devious Nazi plot nearly 50 years after World War II … Deep in a remote mountain settlement, Sam must uncover the village's dark history. If she fails to reach her friend in time, the Nazi survivors will ensure Alfredo's permanent silence. Can Sam blow the lid on the conspiracy before the Third Reich makes a devastating return?

The background to the book is the presence of Nazi war criminals in South America which was often ignored by locals who had fascist sympathies during World War II. Themes such as tacit acceptance of fascism, and local collaboration with fugitives from justice are examined and developed in the context of Sam's constant ability to find herself in the middle of an adventure or mystery.

The Star of Simbako - Book 3

A fabled diamond, a jealous voodoo priestess, disturbing cultural practices. What could possibly go wrong? The third book in the Sam Harris Series sees Sam Harris on her first contract to West Africa to Simbako, a land of tribal kingdoms and voodoo. Nursing a broken heart, Sam Harris goes to Simbako to work in the diamond fields of Fona. She is soon involved with a cast of characters who are starring in their own soap opera, a dangerous mix of superstition, cultural practices, and ignorance (mostly her own). Add a love triangle and a jealous woman who wants her dead and Sam is in trouble again. Where is the Star of Simbako? Is Sam going to survive the chaos?

This book is based on visits made to the Paramount Chiefdoms of West Africa. Despite being nominally Christian communities, Voodoo practices are still part of daily life out there. This often leads to conflicts of interest. Combine this with the horrific ritual of FGM and it makes for a potent cocktail of conflicting loyalties. Sam is pulled into this life by her friend, Adanna, and soon finds herself involved in goings on that she doesn't understand.

The Pink Elephants - Book 4

Sam gets a call in the middle of the night that takes her to the Masaibu project in Lumbono, Africa. The project is collapsing under the weight of corruption and chicanery engendered by management, both in country and back on the main company board. Sam has to navigate murky waters to get it back on course, not helped by interference from people who want her to fail. When poachers invade the elephant sanctuary next door, her problems multiply. Can Sam protect the elephants and save the project or will she have to choose?

The fourth book in the Sam Harris Series presents Sam with her sternest test yet as she goes to Africa to fix a failing project. The day-to-day problems encountered by Sam in her work are typical of any project manager in the Congo which has been rent apart by warring factions, leaving the local population frightened and rootless. Elephants with pink tusks do exist, but not in the area where the project is based. They are being slaughtered by poachers in Gabon for the Chinese market and will soon be extinct, so I have put the guns in the hands of those responsible for the massacre of these defenceless animals.

The Bonita Protocol - Book 5

An erratic boss. Suspicious results. Stock market shenanigans. Can Sam Harris expose the scam before they silence her? It's 1996. Geologist Sam Harris has been around the block, but she's prone to nostalgia, so she snatches the chance to work in Sierramar, her old stomping ground. But she never expected to be working for a company that is breaking all the rules. When the analysis results from drill samples are suspiciously high, Sam makes a decision that puts her life in peril. Can she blow the lid on the conspiracy before they shut her up for good? The Bonita Protocol sees Sam return to Sierramar and take a job with a junior exploration company in the heady days before the Bre-X crash. I had fun writing my first megalomaniac female boss for this one. I have worked in a few junior companies with dodgy bosses in the past, and my only comment on the sector is buyer beware…

Digging Deeper - Book 6

A feisty geologist working in the diamond fields of West Africa is kidnapped by rebels. Can she survive the ordeal or will this adventure be her last? It's 1998. Geologist Sam Harris is desperate for money so she takes a job in a tinpot mining company working in war-torn Tamazia. But she never expected to be kidnapped by blood thirsty rebels.

Working in Gemsite was never going to be easy with its culture of misogyny and corruption. Her boss, the notorious Adrian Black is engaged in a game of cat and mouse with the government over taxation. Just when Sam makes a breakthrough, the camp is overrun by rebels and Sam is taken captive. Will anyone bother to rescue her, and will she still be alive if they do?

I worked in Tamazia (pseudonym for a real place) for almost a year in different capacities. The first six months I spent in the field are the basis for this book. I don't recommend working in the field in a country at civil war but, as for many of these crazy jobs, I needed the money.

Concrete Jungle - Book 7 (series end)

Armed with an MBA, Sam Harris is storming the City - But has she swapped one jungle for another?

Forging a new career was never going to be easy, and Sam discovers she has not escaped from the culture of misogyny and corruption that blighted her field career.

When her past is revealed, she finally achieves the acceptance she has always craved, but being one of the boys is not the panacea she expected. The death of a new friend presents her with the stark choice of compromising her principals to keep her new position, or exposing the truth behind the façade. Will she finally get what she wants or was it all a mirage?

I did an MBA to improve my career prospects, and much like Sam, found it didn't help much. In the end, it's only your inner belief that counts. What other people say, or think, is their problem. I hope you enjoy this series. I wrote it to rid myself of demons, and it worked.

Box Sets

Sam Harris Adventure Box Set Book 2-4
Sam Harris Adventure Box Set Book 5-7
Sam Harris Adventure Box Set Books 2-7

Connect with the Author

About the Author

I write under several pen names and in various genres: PJ Skinner (Travel Adventures and Cozy/Cosy Mystery), Pip Skinner (Sci-Fi), Kate Foley (Irish contemporary), and Jessica Parkin (children's illustrated books).

I moved to the south coast of England just before the Covid pandemic and after finishing my trilogy, The Green Family Saga, I planned the Seacastle Mysteries. I have always been a massive fan of crime and mystery and I guess it was inevitable I would turn my hand to a mystery series eventually.

Before I wrote novels, I spent 30 years working as an exploration geologist, managing remote sites and doing due diligence of projects in over thirty countries. During this time, I collected the tall tales and real-life experiences which inspired the Sam Harris Adventure Series, chronicling the adventures of a female geologist as a pioneer in a hitherto exclusively male world.

I worked in many countries in South America and Africa in remote, strange, and often dangerous places, and loved every minute, despite encountering my fair share of misogyny and other perils. The Sam Harris

Adventure Series is for lovers of intelligent adventure thrillers happening just before the time of mobile phones and the internet. It has a unique viewpoint provided by Sam, a female interloper in a male world, as she struggles with alien cultures and failed relationships.

My childhood in Ireland inspired me to write the Green Family Saga, which follows the fortunes of an English family who move to Ireland just before the start of the troubles.

I have also written a mystery on Mars, inspired by my fascination with all things celestial. It is a science-based murder mystery, think The Martian with fewer potatoes and more bodies.

~~~~~~~~~~~~~~~~~~~~~~~~~~~~~~~~~

Follow me on Amazon to get informed of my new releases. Just put PJ Skinner into the search box on Amazon and then click on the follow button on my author page.

Please subscribe to my Seacastle Mysteries Newsletter for updates and offers by using this QR code

You can also use the QR code below to get to my website for updates and to buy paperbacks direct from me.

You can also follow me on <u>Twitter</u>, Instagram, Tiktok, or on <u>Facebook</u> @pjskinnerauthor

Printed in Great Britain
by Amazon